The Loyal Woman

M.L. Lexi

Titles by M.L. Lexi

The Blind Woman
The Deceitful Woman
The Forgiving Woman
The Grieving Woman
The Guilty Woman
The Loyal Woman
The Noble Woman
The Resolute Woman
The Unfaithful Woman

The Farfalla Family Saga
The Determined Woman
The Persevering Woman
The Invincible Woman

The Fearless Woman Series
The Fearless Woman
The Naïve Woman

Copyright

For every lonely woman. You are not alone.

Fantasy fuels the extinguished fire in us and breathes life into our existence.

—M.L. Lexi

Part I

The Beginning

Loneliness, by its very definition, can't be shared.

—M.L. Lexi

Chapter 1

SOLEDAD THOMAS STARTED her ordinary day by making breakfast for her family, something she had done on hundreds of Mondays. However, today, her day would turn from ordinary to the worst.

White cupboards and tan quartz countertops gleamed under the September sunshine pouring bright through the windows. The smell of frying bacon, scrambled eggs, and toast painted the air. Monday's breakfast menu was always bacon, scrambled eggs, and toast. Consistency was of the utmost importance to Elliot and what he expected of his wife.

Breakfast finished, and the family was off to their busy lives. Elliot was off to carry out his COO duties at Thomas and Partners, his father's accounting firm. The twins, Allie and Annie, and Soledad's youngest, Noah, were off to school to fill their minds with knowledge and teenage angst.

As Soledad did every morning, she watched everyone pile into Elliot's Maserati from the living room window. The usual routine played out precisely as it did every morning. The twins opened the back car doors, always Allie on the right and Annie on the left. Always toss backpacks in, slide into the seats, snap seatbelts in, and set the AirPods in their ears, proceed with head bobbing to the music. Noah got into the front passenger seat, and Elliot behind the wheel. Off they went at eight-fifteen. Always at eight-fifteen. Elliot would drop the children off at school at eight twenty-five, and he would be in his office by eight fifty-five. Always.

Monotony and repetitiveness had become Soledad's life, and Christ, she hated the feeling of boredom and predictability that was her life.

Her family wasn't tedious, her children anything but monotone. Soledad loved her children and husband, and she loved who they were. Or did she?

Doubt had become the essence of her being.

When Elliot turned right on Maple, and the car disappeared, on a long, exhaled breath, Soledad swirled from the window and got on with her humdrum Monday. She had a long list of chores to get to.

First on the day's schedule was laundry, and in the laundry room, Soledad separated, sorted, and tossed the first of many loads she'd do that morning into the washing machine. There was never a shortage of dirty laundry with three fashion-conscious teenagers and a husband.

Soledad was glad Hope and Jasmine, her two eldest, no longer lived at home. As much as Soledad missed them, she was glad they'd moved out when they started university and that independent living stuck after graduation. Two fewer bodies at home took off some of the pressure from her hectic days.

Since birth, Soledad cared for her five children on her own. There had been no nannies, babysitters, or family support. There was no help of any kind. It hadn't been easy. At times, it had been stressful. It was often taxing on the body and mind, but Soledad had done it.

Elliot was the professional, the educated one, the breadwinner. Soledad was the stay-at-home mom, and her job was to care for the children and home and organize her family's lives. Soledad had sacrificed her life to meet their needs. She'd done her part for the past thirty-one years to meet her family's needs and make them happy—at the cost of her happiness.

As much as Soledad loved her children and enjoyed being a mother and wife, her resentment was ready to burst.

Soledad told herself every married woman went through the existential crisis she was going through, and it would pass. It hadn't. The emptiness and disillusion with her life were mounting to distraction, and she feared what she might do. Everyone had a breaking point.

Adding detergent, Soledad turned the dial and set the machine to wash. Her lips curved when Buddy's head spun in chorus with the spin cycle swirling through the glass window. The silly-looking, brown pug with deep wrinkles around the big, dark eyes always put a smile on her face no matter her mood, and this morning's mood was sad and broody.

Today was Soledad's fiftieth birthday, a day she'd dreaded for weeks.

She'd cruised past twenty into thirty without much thought. Her mind was occupied then with marriage and children. She'd inched her way into forty with a hope and a prayer her fiftieth wouldn't come anytime soon. Yet here was her fiftieth birthday, sooner than expected and adding to her feelings of hopelessness.

Soledad hated feeling as she did about a silly birthday, but it was her fiftieth—the worst number in her books.

The big five-oh was the crossover into old age, the time you re-evaluate your life and doubt your choices. It brought on menopause, giving rise to gray hair and hot flashes, a constant reminder of your ageing body. The five-oh brought on dormant disorders and pain you never imagined would touch you. Worse, fifty brought on drooping boobs, the horrors of the turkey neck, and sagging arms, sagging everything.

Soledad's mood was somewhat lifted by the idea of her family coming home tonight. She didn't doubt they would all make it home to surprise her. It was why no one had mentioned her birthday at the breakfast table.

Elliot would show up with a chocolate-chip ice cream cake, the family's favourite and a bouquet of roses. Noah would present her with a bundle of variety-store bought flowers. Hope and Jasmine would override their father's set menu and order Chinese and pizza, and the entire family would gather around the dining room table.

Tonight though, Soledad decided there would be no fast food. With everyone's life going in different directions, it was a rare occasion when her family shared family dinner together, and Soledad planned to make it memorable. She planned to prepare a grand dinner with everyone's favourite foods.

Right now, though, it was time for Buddy's morning walk. The last thing she wanted was a present from Buddy scenting the house.

Walking to the foyer, Soledad looked at herself in the closet door mirror. Her chestnut hair was bound into a messy ponytail. Black leggings designed to smooth out her long legs were paired with a short sleeve Lycra shirt that tightly hugged her body and gave her feminine curves. Except for the gold wedding band on her left hand, she wore no jewellery. She wasn't June Cleaver, and jewelry and housework weren't an ideal match. The same went for makeup, but she needed none. The long, lashed blue eyes, the dainty nose, and delicate pouty mouth on the alabaster face needed no enhancements.

Soledad reached for her pear-yellow running jacket. She slipped on her white running shoes and strapped the running belt that held her water bottle and cell phone around her waist.

Eyeing herself in the mirror, Soledad looked every bit the runner. Too bad she didn't run, hadn't since Hope, her firstborn, came along. Women her age who were mothers and wives, managers of their homes, ran in the movies and fiction novels. Women who were their husband's caterers and hosted the many functions to promote their scaling careers didn't have time to run.

Soledad eyed her screen's phone for the time. Eight-thirty, time for Buddy's half-hour morning walk. Elliot's motto was that schedules made for an efficient life, and he was a stickler for efficiency.

"Buddy, can you pull yourself away from watching the washing to go for your morning walk?" Soledad smiled when Buddy made a mad dash from the laundry room and slid across the polished hardwood and into her. "I thought that would get your attention. Let's get going. We have exactly thirty minutes for your walk. I have a lot to do today." She attached Buddy's leash to his collar as his tail happily thumped against hardwood.

Chapter 2

WHILE BUDDY RAN around the dog park with his friends, a Chihuahua named Thor and a terrier named Fenton, Soledad did a mental check of her To-Do list.

Her mind rolling, Soledad tilted her face up to the sky and let the sun pour over her face. She watched a pair of blue jays wing by and followed the flight of Canada geese in V formation, heading for warmer temperature. Fall was starting to show its face, and the rich hues of rust and gold on the park's trees hinted at the incoming season. That lightened Soledad's mood some. She loved this time of year.

Tonight wouldn't be the usual Monday pasta night. Everyone would get their favourite foods. Feeding six people with different tastes was a challenge. It was the reason Elliot set the daily menus, and everyone had to accept it.

"There are too many varied tastes in this house, and accommodating each one is a burden on you." Elliot had told her. "Set meals will make your life easier."

Who was she to doubt Elliot?

Soledad wasn't a respected doctor like her sister or the COO of a company like her husband. Soledad didn't have the career her children looked up to or aspired to become. She was a homemaker, pure and simple, the guardian of her children. It was her sole contribution, and as such, she'd take care of them to the best of her ability.

When Soledad's phone alarm alerted the end of Buddy's playtime, she tapped it silent and called for him. Thirty minutes went by too fast for Buddy's liking, and it took another fifteen minutes, time Soledad hadn't accounted for in her busy schedule, to coax him home.

Once home, Soledad traded her running belt for her purse. She slung the cross-body bag on and called for Buddy. "Come on, Buddy. We're going for a ride, Buddy."

Buddy's tongue lolling with anticipation in the passenger seat, Soledad backed the car out of the driveway. She was about to floor it when she saw Hazel from her porch, waving her flabby arms as if taking flight to get her attention. Guilt getting the best of Soledad, she stopped the car, rolled her window down, and waited for her eighty-year-old neighbour to shuffle her way toward the car at sloth velocity.

Bent over her walker, Hazel's bright floral dress scraped the pavement. She wore white open-toe sandals with skin tone knee-highs. One sock was wrinkled around her ankle, and the other pulled to her knee.

Foreshadow? Soledad wondered. "Good morning Hazel. I'm making a supermarket run. Do you need anything?"

"Hello, dear, are you going somewhere?" Hazel pushed the thick black-rimmed glasses higher on her nose.

"I'm going to Gino's Market. Can I pick anything up for you?"

Cupping her ear, Hazel leaned in closer. "I'm sorry, dear, can you repeat that? Oh, is that Buddy?"

The old woman couldn't hear much, but Buddy's bark she heard from a mile away. "It is." Soledad rolled the back window down and Buddy put his paws on the windowsill and leaned out.

"Hello, boy. How are you this fine morning?" Hazel delighted the dog with head scratches. "That's a lovely boy. Why don't you come to the house with me? I have treats."

On the invitation, Buddy jumped out the car window like a bullet. "Christ on a bike, not now, Buddy. I don't have time for this." Soledad jumped out of the car. "Get back in the car, Buddy. Hazel needs to get her exercise and take her nap afterward." Soledad gestured Buddy into the front seat. Grudgingly, he jumped in. "He'll come to visit this afternoon, Hazel. Right now, I'm in a bit of a rush."

"Okay, dear. Are you going to the market?"

"I am." Soledad slid behind the wheel.

"Can you pick me up some eggs and milk and..." Hazel raised a finger to her lips and rolled her eyes to the sky as she thought deeply.

"Shit." Soledad pinched the bridge of her nose between her thumb and forefinger.

"What was that, dear?"

"How about I pick up the usual things I get for you?"

"But I may not need them."

"You can pick and choose. I can keep whatever is left over." Soledad strapped herself in.

"I guess we can do that, dear."

"I'll see you later, Hazel," Soledad said, and from the passenger seat, Buddy barked his goodbye.

"Soledad, honey."

"What, what is it, Hazel?" Soledad almost snapped before she caught herself.

"Happy birthday." Hazel's eyes, made to look huge by the thick lens of her glasses, remained riveted on Soledad. "Yes, dear, it's what I wanted to say from the start. My brain doesn't think as well anymore. Anyway, I hope you have a lovely day, dear."

A remorseful smile replaced Soledad's irritation. "Thank you, Hazel," she said and moved on.

The first stop on Soledad's To-Do list was the cleaners to drop off the chocolate suit Elliot needed for the meeting with a highfalutin client in a couple of days. Soledad made an additional note to iron his cobalt shirt and set out the matching silk tie for him to wear.

The next stop was the art supplies store for the Bristol board and Styrofoam spheres Noah needed for his science project. Next on her list was the drug store, where she picked up Elliot's blood pressure prescription and the twins' vitamins.

Soledad drove to Swift Lube for the car's scheduled oil change. She was late for that, but as a loyal customer for decades, Tyrone, the manager, told her she had preferred standing with a wink and snuck her through. That would take a twenty-dollar tip.

Soledad planned to use the thirty minutes her car was in the shop to do her grocery shopping. Kill two birds with one stone. Elliot could never question her efficiency.

Soledad walked three doors down from Swift Lube to Gino's Market. Making her way down the familiar aisles, Soledad picked up everything she needed and a few extra things for Hazel's benefit. Soledad was in the habit of shopping with a prepared list. Elliot had rooted the idea in her that lists were conducive to efficiency and a cost-effective shopping trip, but today, she was winging it.

"I got everyone's favourite food, and won't they be surprised? I got roast beef for Noah and ham for Elliot. The ham bone is for you, Buddy." Buddy's tongue lolled out from the back seat in a canine grin. "For Jasmine and Hope, I got salmon portions and tofu for the twins," Buddy whined at the mention of tofu. "I know, yuck, right? Why the girls would want to eat that stuff is beyond me too?" Soledad said to Buddy, turning onto Main Street.

Next on the list was PetCo to pick up a bag of Buddy's food. "I'm sorry, Buddy, but today you can't come in with me. Today it's an in-and-out visit."

Soledad left an upset Buddy barking in the car, but she had no choice. Buddy would head straight to the toy aisle, and getting him out was an uphill battle, and she had no time for nonsense today. She had to get home to get dinner on the stove.

Buddy forgave Soledad when the car started rolling, and the back window went down. It was two o'clock. As much as her schedule didn't allow it, Soledad couldn't bypass the wine store to pick up a bottle of Riesling Elliot couldn't go without.

"I'll only be a minute, Buddy." The dog's paws planted on the car window, whining, he watched Soledad head into the wine store and return within minutes.

Soledad steered the car for home with the happy thought of her family's visit floating in her mind. Tonight wasn't going to be an echo of past nights.

Chapter 3

THEY DIDN'T COME, not Hope, not Jasmine. Elliot didn't make it home until nine after his usual twelve-hour day at the office. Once home, Elliot barely acknowledged Soledad, picked up a glass and the bottle of Johnnie Walker, and headed into his home office to work some more. Bed followed an hour later. Noah hung out with his hockey teammates after practice, and the twins had dinner with the Conservation Club at Marcello's Pizzeria.

Worse than not making it home for her birthday dinner, no one mentioned it at the breakfast table in the morning. After breakfast, Elliot, Noah, and the twins walked out of her insignificant life into their meaningful ones without saying a word.

Soledad never felt more alone.

Soledad received an email birthday card from her sister Christine, from Africa or whatever God-forsaken place she and her surgeon husband were doing their yearly stint with Doctors Without Borders. No one said anything other than Christine's half-assed but well-meaning birthday wish. No one remembered.

Her parents would have remembered if they weren't long gone, Soledad thought. They always remember.

Untold disappointment flowing in Soledad, she went mushy inside. Sensing Soledad's hurt, Buddy planted his head on her lap. His eyes, all but dripping love and concern, looked up, and it put a smile on her face.

Soledad sniffed back the tears. "You, Buddy, are the best doggie in the world. You always manage to make me feel better." She kissed Buddy's head. In return, Buddy gave Soledad a beaming grin and lapped her face. "And you're also the silliest dog, but now we must get on with the day. We have a lot to do today," she said, setting her sorry feelings aside and crossing from the kitchen to the laundry room.

Tapping the playlist Noah loaded on her phone, Soledad searched through for a song to match her mood. Bill Withers's *Ain't No Sunshine* playing in her ears, Soledad fished the bucket from the supply closet, loaded it with the mop and the necessary cleaning supplies, and turned to the laundry pile.

"Join me in the kitchen when the entertainment is over," Soledad said to Buddy, who remained in the laundry room mesmerized when she set the washing machine to wash the clothes she didn't get yesterday.

In the kitchen, Soledad cleared the breakfast dishes off the table. She washed them, the pan, and the bowl she used to make the pancakes. Tuesday was blueberry pancake day, not banana, not buttermilk, not chocolate chip—never anything other than blueberry. It was what Elliot expected and what she'd done for the thirty-one years of her married life.

Soledad craved excitement, and blueberry pancakes weren't it.

She should have listened to Christine and joined her on her crusade to save humanity. Had she taken heed of her wiser, older sister's words, she would have pursued a medical degree and travelled the world. Soledad would be making her mark on people who'd appreciate her.

But mistakes were made, and our lives took diverging paths when the wrong decisions were made. And here Soledad was.

Soledad wiped down the countertop and stovetop. She mopped the floor until it sparkled. The kitchen spic and span—as Elliot liked—Soledad packed the cleaning supplies into the bucket, grabbed the mop, and started up the stairs. She stopped halfway up when Buddy scrambled past her.

"The washing machine stopped, huh?" Buddy barked his confirmation from the top of the stairs. "Let's go set another load for your entertainment." Buddy's grin wide on his face, he ran down the stairs and slid across the wood floor into the laundry room.

The washing machine spinning, Soledad headed upstairs. She went from room to room, making beds, and cleaning bathrooms. Retrieving the vacuum from the hallway closet, Soledad ran it over rugs as Aretha's voice came through her earbuds.

"R-E-S-P-E-C-T," Soledad chimed in with Aretha and followed with, "A little respect, just a little bit. Damn straight respect," Soledad added before jumping in to croon, "I get tired, just a little bit. Actually, I get tired a lot." Soledad's foot stomped in anger on the vacuum's OFF button and sent Buddy from a leisure stroll into the bedroom to a mad dash under the bed.

"You'd think my husband would remember." Soledad set teeth against temper and tossed the vacuum cleaner with a thump into the closet, and Buddy hid deeper under the bed. "Sorry, Buddy." She slammed the closet door. "I'm not so much angry, but disappointed. You know?"

Buddy peeked his head from under the bed. "It's safe to come out."

Soledad could understand her five children not remembering. At seventeen, Annie and Allie, influenced by Christine's adventures of her travels and the destruction she saw, aimed to become the earth's saviours and the next Greta Thunberg. Annie and Allie's focus was on everything but their mother. As for Noah's forgetfulness, he was a sixteen-year-old boy. Girls, friends, and sports—in that order—were a young boy's nucleus, not his mother.

Soledad understood her eldest daughter's oversight. Hope's pursuits of fulfilling her doctoring dream—again, Christine's influence and not Soledad's—her focus was work and Ethan Sutherland, fellow pediatric resident and live-in boyfriend of three years.

Soledad gave twenty-five-year-old Jasmine the same consideration. Six years Hope's junior, Jasmine's head was buried under the demanding workload at her grandfather's accounting firm. Jasmine's goal was to step into Elliot's shoes and take over the company's management once he inherited it. Dedicating every waking hour to prove herself was where Jasmine's head was.

Soledad gave all of her ambitious children a pass for forgetting, but she couldn't excuse Elliot. "How could he, Buddy? How could he forget my birthday?" she mumbled as she headed down the stairs to the laundry room.

"How could Elliot forget my birthday? Not a call, not even a birthday card. And as for birthday sex, pfft, as if that would happen." She heaved the wet load of clothes from the washing machine to the dryer and lobbed the next load into the washing machine. "Not a 'happy birthday, honey.' A simple happy birthday, Buddy. It's not too much to ask, is it?" Soledad interpreted Buddy's bark as tacit agreement. "Christ on a bike, he could have made an effort. It's my fiftieth." It brought on insecurity and led to her existential crisis.

Back upstairs in her bedroom, Soledad looked at the eyes in the mirror over the dressing table, staring at her. "I feel as old as I look." She yanked the earbuds out of her ears and tossed them onto the bed.

Soledad was an optimist by nature, but her life and marriage had been verging on boring for so long that she was at the point of no return. How could she not be when the loneliness had encased her like a tight blanket for too long? Loneliness felt worse than the sadness that came with it. Loneliness, by its very definition, can't be shared. Sadness could.

Soledad wasn't demanding or unreasonable. She recognized Elliot's work responsibilities. It sustained their family. She even empathized with Elliot's desperate need for his father's validation. As the successor to Thomas and Partners—the accounting firm the over-achieving Charles Winston Thomas built from the ground up—the pressure on Elliot to prove himself to his demanding father was overwhelming.

Soledad accepted her children, getting on with their lives. A timely assertion of the truest adage known to humankind was life goes on. Still, Soledad couldn't help but feel sorry for herself, like a footnote to her family's life.

The sadness leaked out as the misery pushed in.

Soledad didn't hate her life. It was that life wasn't living up to her expectations. She wanted more of one, needed more out of life.

Soledad never regretted opting to raise her children over pursuing her dancing career—her true love. She'd trained for ballet since she could walk and had dreamt of becoming the next Sylvie Guillem on the stage, but electing to be a wife and mother was the right decision. It was then as it was three decades later. As rewarding as being a wife and mother was, there was a void in her that needed fulfillment.

Fire in her life and bed was what Soledad needed in her life.

Maybe it was the onset of mid-life hitting, burnout or the impending empty nest syndrome crushing down on her.

Hope and Jasmine rarely came home anymore or bothered to call. Soledad saw that look in Hope's eyes for Ethan that a woman gets for the man she plans to walk her down the aisle. Hope was already lost to her work and Ethan and in time, she would be lost to her family. Jasmine wasn't far behind, and the twins would soon be off to university to save the world or wherever the feeling of the day took them.

As for Noah, the boy liked his independence.

Perhaps Soledad's loneliness stemmed from the lack of intimacy and lack of emotion she and Elliot hadn't shared in what felt like forever. They claimed men were the sexual ones, Not Elliot. Debits and credits got him more excited than Soledad ever could.

Whatever the reason, Soledad had an itch she needed scratching, and Elliot wasn't doing it.

She craved attention, a night of wild, uninhibited sex. Elliot was a loyal husband, but Soledad couldn't remember the last time she and Elliot had sex, let alone when the last time was that Elliot made her toes curl in bed. Elliot had never been a toe-curling type lover, but she'd enjoy the connection, the intimacy of touch. Soledad had long forgotten what it was to be kissed, held passionately, and told she was loved.

It had been too long since there had been whispered romanticisms between them. Those had gone by the wayside shortly after their marriage when Soledad and Elliot became comfortable. The goodbye kisses, the I love you, and passionate moments shared between husband and wife had gone the way of the Dodo—extinct.

Soledad took part of the blame. She'd shrugged off passion as something no longer as important when Hope came along. A young nineteen, Soledad was overwhelmed by a baby, motherhood, and running a household. By the time Noah arrived, Soledad's concentration was on the children. So absorbed was Soledad with their nurturing she failed to grasp the magnitude of how she and Elliot were drifting into separate lives.

Wasn't that what happened to all couples? Soledad wondered. Marriage wasn't like what Soledad grew up watching on television. The foundation of the flawless Cleaver family was as farcical as the pearls around June's neck.

Her insecurity was playing a part in the downfall of her marriage.

She wasn't the slim ballet dancer of her teens. She'd bore five children, and stretch marks and a saggy tummy were an unavoidable evil. She'd eaten a few too many carbs over the years, which showed in the twenty-five-pound weight gain. It didn't help that her morning runs had gone by the wayside after the children came. That didn't mean she was primed to be put out to pasture. She was a young fifty-year-old virile woman with a few years left.

If only Elliot could see that. A woman liked the music of lovemaking with the man she loved.

Wishing things were different, Soledad stepped into the shower and let the hot water rain down on the tears that began to fill her eyes. As hard as she tried to hold the tears back, they began to flow unchecked. Cried empty, Soledad stepped out of the shower and wrapped her wet body into a white towel.

Walking into her bedroom, Soledad's red-rimmed eyes curved into a soft smile when Buddy aimed loving eyes her way, and his tail crazily thumped on the bed when he saw her.

"If everyone were as doting as you, I wouldn't feel so blah." Soledad fell back on the bed next to Buddy, who cuddled with her, and stared at the ceiling. "I'll tell you a secret, Buddy. This empty feeling chokes me and makes my mind wander, and I'm afraid of what I may do."

Chapter 4

"MOM, WE'RE HOME." Noah's hair was damp with sweat, and his face flushed red with excitement and heat from the hockey game he'd played against the Devils. He dropped his equipment bag on the foyer and bent down to give Buddy a head scratch when he ran up to greet him and Elliot. "Did you see how I clapped that last goal into the net? Slap shot right between their legs, past the goalie and into the net. Score Thomas" Noah swung the imaginary hockey stick, reliving the moment.

"It was a great move, bud. You caught Dad's eye and a prouder grandfather he couldn't be. And ditto for me." Elliot closed the front door and dropped his key on the console table. "Soledad, come congratulate your hockey-star son on the great game he played." Elliot shrugged out of his jacket, and Noah followed suit.

"I'm going to wash up." Noah took the hanger Elliot handed him after chucking his jacket on the floor.

"Don't take too long. We leave in half an hour, text your sisters to let them know." Elliot loosened his tie and unbuttoned the top two on his shirt. "Soledad, where the hell are you?" Elliot called out again.

"You know, I'd rather have pizza at Marcello's to celebrate than...." Buddy barked in agreement at the sound of pizza.

"This dog has to be part Italian."

Noah hooted a laugh. "You do love your pizza, don't you, boy? Me too. Do we need to go to that fancy-ass restaurant Grandfather insists on taking us to celebrate my win?" Noah hung up his jacket in the closet.

Elliot, too, would prefer to sit at a booth at Marcello's Pizzeria with a large pepperoni rather than be in the stuffy, uppity steak house his father insisted on putting Noah on display for his cronies. Life wasn't always about getting what you wanted.

"We don't want to spurn your grandfather's generous gesture." Charles Winston Thomas wouldn't take that well, and the last thing Elliot needed was the added stress of an irate father on his back. "Text Allie and Annie to get their butts home in the next ten minutes. Soledad, where are you?"

"Do they have to come, Dad? Isn't it enough that I have to eat medium-rare steak and potatoes, 'the food of champions,' as Grandfather puts it, without having to endure a save-the-world talk while eating raw meat?"

"I could do without the lecture too, but as their father, I have a legal obligation to feed them." Elliot gave his son a wink. "Go on, text them while I go up to change. Soledad," Elliot called out again. "Your mother is not in the bedroom or bathroom. She's nowhere to be found up here," Elliot said as he went from room to room. "Check in the kitchen."

"Nope, she's not down here," Noah called out, opening the refrigerator door and reaching for a pop can.

"How could she not be? Check in the laundry room." Elliot's voice now sounded edgy.

"She's not here, Dad." Noah casually sipped on his pop and plopped himself on the kitchen table.

Elliot raced down the stairs and into the kitchen. "She has to be. She always is." Elliot opened the pantry door and poked his head in.

"What do you have there, Buddy?" Noah reached for the envelope Buddy had in his mouth. "Umm, Dad."

"Text your mother, ask her where the hell she is. She knew we were doing dinner with Dad tonight." Elliot said in a huff and called for Soledad again. "Soledad, where the hell are you?"

"Mom's not home, Dad. She's gone."

"Dad's not going to be happy about this. Where would she go?"

Soledad was always home, morning, noon, and night. She was always there for dinnertime. She had no friends, and her only family, her sister, was thousands of miles away.

Elliot took the note Noah held out and read it. "Shit."

"Shit, indeed." Noah looked Elliot directly in the eye. "She's left us."

Chapter 5

AIR THICK WITH heat and moisture hit Soledad when she stepped off the plane onto the tarmac. The day's blue sky faded to black as the sun slipped out of sight for the night and a sliced, white moon rose in the west. Palm trees bulging with coconuts stretching to the sky swayed in a light Caribbean breeze. Soledad caught the salty taste and smell of the ocean and the drift of a burning joint. Bob Marley's voice floated from somewhere in the island's depths, telling everyone not to worry about a thing.

The crowd that descended the plane with Soledad was loud with holiday chatter. They wore colourful shorts and flowered short-sleeved shirts and flowing pastel-coloured sundresses. Men wore baseball hats, and the women wide-brimmed straw hats. All flashed their cell phone cameras to memorialize the moment, were rowdy and jubilant, and set to begin their dream vacation.

Soledad didn't share in their jubilation. Whether from guilt or shame, Soledad's belly jittered with nerves. Responsible, cautious Soledad, who always put her family before her own needs, had never done anything as irresponsible or adventurous as board a plane to an unknown island alone.

Soledad was as conservative as they came. At twenty, when Soledad met Elliot, she was a never-been-kissed virgin. Elliot was her first everything. They married two years later, and Soledad went from her parents' home to Elliot's. There was never anything in between. Soledad didn't experience independent living or hold a job outside of running her home. And here she was on Topaz Island, alone with her family, who had no clue where she was.

The winds of change, Soledad thought. "All I can do now is deal with what's in front of me," she told herself, reaching for her carry-on and suitcase.

"Welcome to Topaz Island." His voice flowed with an Italian accent as warm as the drifting wind.

He was tall and gorgeous. His windblown black hair curled carelessly around a deeply tanned face with thick lips and large, mysterious dark eyes. He wore an emerald green shirt and khaki pants that traced the powerfully built body beneath it. At his sockless feet were tan Fendi loafers. He was male perfection and every woman's fantasy.

"Thank you." Soledad lifted her eyes to meet the dazzling dark eyes against the honey-brown of his skin.

"I understand you are a last-minute booking," he said, studying the skittish woman under the streetlamp casting a pool of light over them.

A cloud of honey-brown hair spilled around an unpainted face with few lines at the corners of her mouth and the brilliant blue eyes. She was inches shorter than his six-foot frame, with some meat on her bones that added to her curvy body. He liked that. The pencil-thin look was a falsehood ingrained into women by the fashion industry. Men wanted something to grab. She wore jeans, tight and faded, a mauve, flowing blouse tucked at the waist and flat patent shoes. The vulnerable femininity she exuded was alluring.

"May I see your ticket, please?"

Soledad's guard promptly went up. "Why? Why do you want to see my ticket?" Probing glacial blue eyes fixed on him.

"To find out what bus you are to board that will take you to your resort, of course."

A slow flush worked its way up her throat to her cheeks. "Yes, of course. Sorry, you're not wearing a uniform."

"The regular welcoming director could not make it. I am a last-minute fill-in, Carlo Moretti." He took the ticket Soledad dug from her tote. "You are staying at the Paradise Resort, Miss Thomas," Carlo said after examining the ticket.

"Yes … ummm …. about the Miss." Soledad reconsidered correcting him.

"Yes." His expression was benign, but his dominating presence unpredictably made Soledad's brain freeze. For an interminable fifteen seconds, the silence drifted. "You were saying, Miss Thomas."

"Nothing, I was saying nothing." Soledad's voice was a whisper.

"Please, you board bus number five. It will take you to the resort. It will be a short fifteen-minute ride." Carlo handed her ticket back.

"Okay, thank you."

"It's the other way, Miss Thomas." He pointed a finger in the opposite direction.

Gasping, Soledad stopped and turned. "Yes, of course. About the Miss thing."

"Excuse me, you prefer, Ms. Thomas?" Carlo emphasized the S in Ms. "I like a progressive, beautiful woman setting me straight."

Soledad's cheeks took on a faint tint of pink at the unexpected compliment. "I ... ah ... need to get to my bus."

Carlo waved her through and turned to follow her.

"Why are you following me?" Her voice was panicked, and her look was cagey as she scanned around her to make sure there were enough people to offer a protective hand if the need arose.

"I...." was Carlo's only word before she cut him off.

"If you don't stop following me, I'll scream for the police," she said, taking a few steps forward. When he also did, Soledad stopped in her tracks. Round eyes narrowed to thin slits. "I warned you to stop following me."

The fire in her eyes had his glands doing a joyful jig. "But I must, Ms. Thomas."

"No, no, you mustn't," she snapped with the ferocity of a lioness.

She was a firecracker, Carlo thought. He flashed a warm smile to counter her piercing gaze. "I must follow you because I am also your bus driver. This is our bus. Welcome aboard, Ms. Thomas." Carlo's mouth tipped up at the corners as he put his hand out to help her up.

Smart-ass, she thought, latching onto her suitcase and lugging it up the steps.

Chapter 6

ELLIOT FOUND SOLEDAD'S dresser drawers were empty, and her closet was cleared of most of her clothes. He got the worry line between his eyebrows reserved for his daughters' escapades when he found Soledad's suitcase gone.

Elliot stepped away from the closet and fell back on the edge of the bed. Forgetting Soledad's birthday wasn't a minor blunder. She was gone. Elliot closed his eyes and let his thoughts drift back to piece together what had led to her abrupt departure.

She never led me to believe she was unhappy.

Had she?

Elliot rose to pace.

No, no, she hadn't. Bewilderment was replaced with annoyance. *Christ, how could you, Soledad? How could you leave her children and me without a word?*

Elliot paced some more, thinking, trying to pinpoint signs Soledad sent to indicate she was unhappy. He couldn't think of any because there had been none. Soledad hadn't expressed discontent or complained.

Why would she? Her life is as complete as it could be. Wasn't it? *Maybe I work more than I should, but Soledad understands it's for her and the kids that I put in so many hours. She knows it's for our future.*

Elliot ran a frustrated hand through his hair.

Goddamn it. She's never worked a day in her life. I made sure of that, and this is the thanks I get.

Sure, Elliot wasn't as attentive as he should be, and yes, romance was nonexistent between Soledad and him, but the pressures of work weighed too heavily to focus on mundane issues. They'd been married long enough to have crossed beyond the romance and passionate phase of their relationship.

Then there were the financial demands as the sole supporter of seven people.

Being at home all day, without the pressures of work and everything that came with it, under a demanding father who expected perfection, you wouldn't understand that, Soledad.

Elliot's focus was his family's comfort, financial stability, a well-funded retirement account, and a roof over their heads. There was the education fund for the twins and Noah, who would soon head to university. Tuition, room and board didn't come cheap. Soledad should know that from experience.

Elliot was pacing a trench in the bedroom carpet.

He could smell Soledad's scent. It was all around him. The vision of Soledad lying on her side of the bed, next to him flashed at him. There was such comfort knowing she was there with him every night. He might not have told her as much, but he always felt as if he could breathe more deeply when she was around.

Elliot could trust her with the children. After all, Soledad had moulded their children into the responsible, independent people they were. Soledad made Elliot the man he was. He was the man he was because of her.

The gut punch to his stomach at the thought Soledad wouldn't be there anymore made his chest constrict as if there was a heavy weight pressing against it. Elliot fell back on the bed.

"Why didn't you talk to me, Soledad? I'm not a mind reader. No man is. We don't understand the mechanics of a woman's mind or their thought process. For as long as man has been on this earth, we never have been able to crack a woman's mind, and I expect we never will. I can't figure out what you're thinking. Where are you, Soledad?"

The pressure pressed down on his chest, and panic set in when he couldn't shake the nagging feeling of conclusion. The thought made him nauseous down to the pit of his stomach.

"I need to find Soledad. I need to go after her." Elliot shot to his feet. Noah, get your laptop. I need your help."

Chapter 7

Wednesday, September 9, Morning

CARLO WALKED INTO the open dining room, bursting with the morning breakfast crowd. The smell of coffee hung in the air. Over the hum of conversation, the clink of cutlery on plates, and the rattling of ice against glass drifted the sound of rhythmic music from the overhead speakers. Birds hopeful for food scraps flitted above the diners' heads.

The sea was a bold blue looking to the horizon, and the sky equalled in hue under a brightly shining sun. On the beach, sun worshippers spread out on lounge chairs. Their bodies glowed under a layer of suntan lotion.

The wind blew strands of long, dark hair enhancing the dark smiling eyes. His fashionable stubble was freshly trimmed. His white cotton shirt, sleeves rolled to the elbows, traced broad shoulders and strong muscular arms. With him, he brought the sweet smell of his cologne.

Every woman in the room watched him in silence, admiring the fit of his tan chinos on a tight butt and long legs. Carlo wasn't interested in any of those women. There was only one woman he was intent on seeing, and he immediately spotted her sitting alone at a table drinking coffee and watching the roll of foamy waves lapping the shore.

Greeting guests, Carlo casually wound his way past the long line of people queuing at the buffet and around the dozens of tables scattered throughout the room. "Good morning, Ms. Thomas. How was your first night with us?"

Soledad looked up over the rim of her cup to meet the luminous black pools smiling at her. "Good, thank you."

"I didn't see you at dinner or any of our bars last night." His breathy Italian accented voice flowed musically and had Soledad's insides liquefying.

"I, ah, stayed in my room." Pacing and wondering what I've done and what I'm doing here without Elliot and my children.

What was she thinking packing up and charging out of the house midway through the day to hop on a flight headed thousands of miles from her home—by herself? She hadn't left a note or let anyone know where she was going or how long she'd be gone.

Soledad's guilt at leaving the children and Elliot had too many thoughts tumbling around in her head all night, too much guilt. Her fired-up brain and churning stomach had kept her awake all night. At one point, Soledad came close to calling home. When she didn't follow through, she dialled the front desk instead and asked to book her a ticket home on the next flight. Liquid courage from the complimentary rum bottle she found in the mini-refrigerator stopped her rethinking and going through with it.

She was here for herself, for some much-needed time to regroup and decide what she wanted from life because what she had at home wasn't working anymore.

"You missed a good party," Carlo's said.

Christ, did he have to look so good early in the morning? "I was tired and not in the mood for a party." Soledad dropped her cup on the table when the thought struck and said, "Wait. Are you stalking me? I'll report you to the resort."

"May I?" Carlo gestured to the empty seat across from her.

"No, you may not. Answer me. Are you stalking me?" Soledad demanded, struggling to stop her mind from running to places she didn't want it to go.

"You appear a little bit agitated, Ms. Thomas." He held his index finger and thumb wide apart to indicate the extent of her distress. "Maybe we should get you off the coffee, *si*?"

"No." She held tightly onto the cup when Carlo reached for it.

"You are a strong one."

"Let go of my cup." The cold, steely glint of those blue eyes had him releasing his grip on the cup. "I'm still waiting for an answer." Soledad drummed impatient fingers on the table.

"I should introduce myself. That may clear things up. My name is Carlo Moretti." His voice was so mild in contrast to Soledad's ire that she stiffened.

"We established that yesterday, and it clears nothing up." Her jaw was set tight.

He loved fire in a woman, and she had a red-hot flame going. "I am the resort owner, and I make it a point to know all my guests." Soledad's angry embarrassment made her cheeks take on a tint of pink. "No need for apologies."

"I wasn't apologizing."

"I try to get behind that."

Her brows knit in confusion and straightened when she figured out what he meant. "You mean in front of it."

"My English is not so good, *perché sono italiano e parlo la lingua dell'amore,*" he said with an Italian intonation hat made her insides melt and left her staring at him. "I said because I am Italian and speak the language of love."

"Yes, of course, you did."

"Shall we start again, Ms. Thomas? My name is Carlo Moretti, and I welcome you to my resort." Carlo reached for her hand and kissed it.

A tingle skittered up and down Soledad's spine. "Yes, well, thank you, Mr. Moretti."

"My friends call me Carlo. May I join you?"

From the attention he was attracting from every woman in the room, a man like him had no shortage of friends. Men like Carlo Moretti thrived on the sexual conquests they notched on their bedposts. Well, he had a surprise coming his way. Soledad wasn't about to become one of his statistics.

"No, you may not, and I'm not your friend."

His lips, firm and full, curved. "You could be."

Soledad sunk back in her chair. "I'm not here to make friends, Mr. Moretti."

"Why are you here, Ms. Thomas?"

"To—" Her eyes went contemplative. "I'm here to find answers, Mr. Moretti."

"Carlo, Mr. Moretti sounds so impersonal. Maybe I can help you with that." He slid into the chair next to her. "You know, finding the answers you are looking for."

"No, you cannot, Mr., umm, Carlo." Soledad corrected when he raised a finger to point out her slip. "What you can help me with is to tell me how you pin-pointed me missing from amongst the four hundred guests here."

"Five hundred and, Ms. Thomas...."

"Soledad, since we're on first name terms."

"That is a beautiful name. It means solitude. I certainly hope that is not what you are looking for. It would be a shame for a beautiful woman such as yourself to want to hide away."

And she was beautiful. Her hair was tied back this morning, setting off her large eyes, the colour of shining sapphires, and those kissable lips were begging to be kissed. She wore a white lace sundress with cheery sunflowers. But it was her vulnerable femininity, some of which he'd already seen last night, that charmed him.

Soledad's brow shot up. "That's a poor-ass line."

He threw back his head and laughed. "It is not a line, Soledad. I believe beautiful women should share the wealth, let the world feast on their beauty."

Was this what they called flirting? Soledad wondered. Soledad had long forgotten what flirting was, how it felt to be complimented and made to feel attractive. Still, she kept her guard up. The man was too skilled and charismatic not to raise the warning flag.

Carlo's eyes held hers a beat too long, and Soledad felt an unexpected twinge of nervousness. "To answer your question, Soledad, I make it a point to know all the beautiful women at my resort."

"Good morning, Mr. Moretti. May I pour you a coffee and get you your usual breakfast?" The waitress sidled to the table with a steaming pot of java in hand. The tag pinned to the left pocket of her white, short sleeve shirt read Mariela. She had enviably smooth coffee-coloured skin, and her hair was tied tightly into a bun. The playful look in her large, dark eyes told Soledad she wanted to do more than pour Carlo coffee.

"Thank you, Mariela, but I will take a mimosa. You know how I like it."

The young girl flashed a dazzling smile that twinkled white against her ebony skin. "Heavy on the champagne and light on the orange juice."

"You know me so well, darling," Carlo said with a wink. "The lady will also have a mimosa, but best make hers a regular pour."

"Of course, Mr. Moretti. Coming right up, Mr. Moretti." Mariela flew off like a whirlwind toward the bar.

"She certainly aims to please."

"She is an employee of mine, not a lover," Carlo said, causing Soledad's slash of dark eyebrow to rise. "It is what you were thinking, *si*?" His words tapered off to a grin.

"No. That was the furthest thing from my mind, and that's your business." Soledad picked up her coffee cup and held it between her hands to keep her nervous hands busy.

From the overhead speakers, a reggae rendition of *Under The Boardwalk* replaced the melodic bachata. The ping and pong of balls bouncing against the table chimed in when two boys picked up the paddles to challenge one another.

"You should never turn down the compliment from a man who finds you attractive, Soledad," he said in a way that made her heart jitter around in her chest. The reawakening of a feeling she hadn't felt in a long while.

"I'm married with a husband." Soledad tossed out the foolish comment.

"Husband, wife, lover, it is all good with me."

"I have five children. Five grown children," she added as a defence mechanism to the unexpected attraction rising in her for Carlo.

"Respect for how you have maintained your splendour. Is that the right word?"

As if he didn't know, Soledad mused. Men like him were suave with the tongue.

"Here you are, Mr. Moretti." Mariela walked up and set the mimosas on the table.

The smile Carlo shot Mariela before she moved on to serve her next order sent her mind churning wild tales to tell her coworkers.

"She's tumbled into love," Soledad said.

"Until the next man to aim a smile in her direction." Carlo made a smirk twist Soledad's lips. "You say you are married, but I did not see Mr. Thomas with you."

"This resort of yours is impressive and beautiful." Soledad dodged, she knew it, and he knew it. "And you're so young."

Fishing, he thought, smiling to himself. "I am thirty-two, and I am single. I am Italian, but I spend my winters on the island. This resort, the hotel, the restaurants, bars, and twenty miles of luxurious white sand beachfront, are mine. I earned all this the old-fashioned way. I inherited it from my grandmother, who got it from her fourth husband and island magnate. You may say she too inherited the old-fashioned way." Carlo commented with a wink.

Soledad's eyes crinkled with a smile. Her first for him, and he realized his accomplishment.

"Now that you know all about me, will you continue to dodge my question?" He watched her cross her legs; there was a lot of leg to watch.

"I'm not dodging," she said defensively.

Carlo sank back in his chair and sipped on his mimosa. "Is your husband joining you later? I require the information purely for security reasons."

Of course, he did. "He's supposed to be." Soledad's lips pressed together for a moment giving the lie away.

"I'll add him to the guest list. What's his name?"

Soledad slipped into a moment of silence to gather the strength to say, "Don't bother," and sighed under her breath. "He's not coming. He couldn't get away from work. He has a very important job." He won't even notice I'm gone for hours. "I made the trip on my own to do some … thinking." Soledad looked off and away.

There was something so sad resonating in her eyes, and Carlo laid a hand over Soledad's. When she didn't pull away, he squeezed her hand to help smooth away the hurt in her eyes. It was a light touch, a fleeting connection, but it offered the comfort, sympathy, and understanding Soledad didn't get from Elliot anymore.

Soledad thought about that for a moment. A mere physical stimulus from a hand touch put a fire in her belly she hadn't felt in so long. How desperate had she become for human connection that a touch from a total stranger had emotions stirring in her?

Soledad's heart pounded so fast in her chest that it felt like it was trying to smash open her ribcage and escape. Carlo had Soledad's mind racing to places it shouldn't. She had to get control of herself. A momentary lapse of control could be life-changing. It could destroy her family and marriage, but it could bring excitement into her life. There was no doubt that Carlo Moretti would fill her life with the excitement it lacked.

In her paranoia, Soledad imagined Carlo had read her mind. "Stop staring at me." Soledad yanked her hand from his grip.

"Will I see you on the beach later? We are planning a luau for lunch. Will you join?"

They'd only just met, but the intractable connection with him was undeniable. Carlo gave her the listening ear she didn't have in Elliot. Being with Carlo would be liberating and exhilarating. With him, Soledad could allow her darkest thoughts and feelings to surface without fear of censure or dismissal.

"We will serve too many tropical drinks, roast a pig on a spit, and offer much fun. For the discriminating palate, we will offer hamburgers and hot dogs." That put a smile on Soledad's face. "Join us. If not to enjoy the party, come to help me. I can use the helping hand of a beautiful woman." Carlo left the statement suspended in the quiet space between them.

Chapter 8

AWAKE ALL NIGHT, Elliot needed to jump-start his groggy brain. Like a man sleepwalking, he dragged himself from his office to the kitchen, dug a bag of coffee out of the cupboard, and filled the espresso maker. Turning the flame on the stove, he set the coffee maker on the stove to brew. Making coffee was the extent of his cooking capability, and it would be breakfast.

Elliot was calm while waiting for the coffee to brew, even if worry and panic had twin grips on his throat. Last night, nothing had come up from Noah's scour of Soledad's search history on her laptop. There was no hotel booking or car rental uncovered. Nothing.

After searching through Soledad's laptop for three hours, Noah fell asleep on the computer's keyboard bringing Elliot's desperate search for Soledad to a halt. Reluctantly, Elliot sent Noah to bed to rest his brain. He needed Noah to be alert.

The coffee spurted and filled the chamber, and Elliot poured into a cup and drank. With three espressos in him, Elliot poured a fourth cup and was about to walk back to the office when Noah walked into the kitchen to the strong scent of coffee in the air.

"Any of that coffee left?" Noah's hair was finger-combed back. He wore jeans and running shoes. His white T-shirt displayed the words Gaming Legend in black, bold letters across the front.

"No. You shouldn't drink coffee. It stunts your growth. Grab some cereal and meet me in the office. I'll be waiting for you."

"Ah, Dad, I have school."

"Not today, you don't. We need to find your mother." Elliot tossed back the coffee and started out of the kitchen.

The smirk of pleasure twisted Noah's lips. "Whatever you say, Dad." Aside from sports, school was a complete waste of time.

Ten minutes later, with Elliot watching over Noah's shoulder, they were back on Soledad's laptop. Although Elliot didn't think Soledad had done anything as crazy as to take a last-minute flight to an unknown destination, he had Noah check.

"You need to find something, Noah. Any little detail, no matter how inconsequential, might lead somewhere."

"I told you, Dad, I've set the laptop to automatically delete all history, cookies, everything, on shutdown." Noah tapped on the keyboard.

"Why would you do that?" Elliot asked to test his son because the answer was obvious. The boy was verging into manhood, and exploring sites he didn't want anyone to know about was what teenage boys did. Elliot understood the boy.

Elliot would never admit it aloud, but the boy was his favourite of his children. He and Noah were cut from the same cloth, similar in many ways. Elliot understood his son's mindset, as he never would his daughters no matter how hard he tried. The working of a woman's mind was every man's kryptonite.

Noah chose from the dozen excuses that ran through Noah's head, "The twins were jamming it up with makeup vids and stupid environmental stuff searches, too much bullshit to cache."

Elliot cocked a brow. The boy never hesitated to throw his sister's under the bus. "That's the best you can do?"

"I'm working here, Dad." Noah tapped on the keyboard some more.

"Where the hell has your mother gone?"

"You know you'll have to tell Dumb and Dumber upstairs about mom's disappearance. The twins aren't that bright, but they are needy, and they'll be missing Mom's cooking, her cleaning services, and everything she does for them. They can't survive without Mom."

Elliot thought about that and concluded that, right there, was why Soledad left. They all saw Soledad as their maid, cook, chauffeur, and a girl Friday. How did he not see what he now saw as clear as day? He and the children had taken Soledad for granted all these years.

There were so many things they, he, should have done differently. Elliot tried to remember the last time he told her how much he appreciated everything he did for them.

He couldn't remember.

Soledad wasn't the bouquet-of-roses type of woman, but he could have made an effort to take her out to one of those bars she liked and endured the noise for her. Soledad was an excellent cook and loved to cook for the family. She had gone as far as to take cooking classes at the local culinary school for the family's benefit. Still, Elliot could have occasionally spared Soledad from kitchen duty and treated her to dinner now and then. He should have given as much as she gave. Foresight was twenty-twenty.

The goddamn pressures of work, his father's expectations, and demands blinded Elliot to what was going on at home. He let Soledad down, the only person who asked nothing of him and devoted herself to making his and their children's lives better.

Soledad never complained, wasn't a demanding wife, or put excess pressure on him as many of his colleagues' wives did. Outdoing the Joneses by making more money, status, a bigger house, private school for Johnny, and exotic vacations, were some of the demands wives put on their work-stressed husbands. Not Soledad.

Soledad didn't demand the outrageous from Elliot. She always stretched a dollar to the fullest and raised their children to reflect the admirable values that made him proud to be their father.

She was the perfect wife and a good mother. Elliot sighed under his breath. Soledad deserved better than the half-assed effort he put into their marriage.

Soledad was the best of him, and Elliot couldn't lose her.

He couldn't bear the thought. Panic crushed Elliot's chest and shut off his air.

"Did you find anything, Noah? A clue, a lead, anything at all? We need to find your mother," Elliot snapped.

Noah clicked open the following browser and checked the history, and it too was wiped clean. "Shit, Nothing. I have one more place to check."

"You're going into her email account?" Elliot questioned when Noah clicked the sign-in screen to life.

"Do you want me to help or not?"

"How do you even know her username and passcode?"

Noah slanted a look over his shoulder. "Mom wouldn't even know how to flip open the laptop if it wasn't for me. I'm the one who set the account up for her."

Elliot watched Noah type the password, Soledad's name followed by his birthday, and pressed enter. "And I'm assuming you never go in there to read her emails."

"Why would I want to read emails from her book club, Buddy's groomer, or Aunt Christine's insane medical adventures? You know Aunt Christine and Uncle Colin are insane. They're in the Congo right now." Noah's fingers tapped at light speed on the keyboard. "Who voluntarily goes to the Congo?"

Elliot's eyebrows raised evenly. "We'll discuss this later. Are you in?"

"Voila!" Noah said when the emails flashed on the screen.

"Look for an email confirming a hotel, a car rental booking, anything of the sort," Elliot instructed, watching Noah surf through the emails.

"Nothing, but she could have trashed it." Noah clicked on the trash file. "Nope, nothing interesting in the trash, but this may help." Noah pointed to the email that read Your Mastercard statement is available. "I set it up for her to receive her statements via email and know the access codes for the site. I can also access her bank account. I have those codes too."

"Of course you do," Elliot muttered.

"I'll sign in, and we can check the charges posted to the Mastercard statement and her bank account in the last twenty-four hours." Noah slanted a look over his shoulder at Elliot. "That is unless you don't want me to."

Elliot sighed, then set his lips firmly. "Go ahead, but we're still having a chat about access."

A smile creased one corner of Noah's mouth. "Whatever you say, Dad," he said and proceeded to peck industriously on the keyboard.

Chapter 9

SOLEDAD'S CONVERSATION WITH Carlo at the breakfast table prompted an escape to her room. The cleaner had already been, and the smell of Pine-Sol hung thick in the air. The blue bedspread with large red poppies on the king-size bed was neatly tucked in place, and pillows were plumped and laid side-by-side up against the headboard. The curtain was drawn open, and from the eastward-looking sliding glass door, a prism of light cut through and made the room with pink-washed walls and Talavera Mexican tiled floor shine bright.

Soledad picked up the television converter on the night table next to bed and flipped to the weather channel. The seven-day forecast called for sun, blue skies, and heat for the next seven days. Perfect bathing suit weather, Soledad thought, falling on her back on the bed. If only she had the confidence to be seen in one.

As much as the extra twenty-five pounds she carried was evenly allocated on her body, Soledad wouldn't dare put it on display in a bathing suit for public consumption. She questioned her decision to escape to a beach destination over a European bus tour.

From somewhere on the beach, the faint murmur of rhythmic percussion and bass from reggae music flowed, and Soledad was reminded of why she chose the beach destination.

Soledad muted the television and ran the play-by-play of her exchange with Carlo at breakfast. Was Carlo flirting with her? Her.

It had been so long since her flirting days that she didn't know what passed for it anymore. There had to be nuances in the seduction game since her teen years. Christ, she hoped so.

In the end, Soledad determined no way sizzling-hot Carlo was interested in a woman fighting age and weight. The man had the pick of the crop from any of the ravening women that eyed him when he walked into the dining room. Christ, she thought they were ready to pounce her when he bypassed them and walked to her table.

Soledad had to admit she liked the resentment in their eyes. She couldn't deny basking in the attention of a younger man she never imagined would give her a second thought. Feeling desirable, beautiful, and young at her age was a welcomed sensation. Soledad revelled in the idea of a man decades younger awakening long-dormant feelings. It felt great.

A compliment and attention from a man to a lonely woman was all it took for Soledad to dangle on the fine line between respectability and impropriety.

Passing a weary hand over her face, Soledad rose to pace the room. "Really, Soledad, you're a married woman and mother. You shouldn't be taking pleasure in the man's attention. Being here alone is a huge mistake," Soledad told the reflection coming at her from the mirror over the dressing table.

She wasn't one to fuss about her appearance. Yet, Soledad had fussed with her hair in the past hour, debated between sandals or flip-flops, makeup or not. The clothes she'd debated wearing to the luau were piled on the bed.

In the end, Soledad settled for the salmon lace-up cami dress and white gladiator sandals. She applied eyeliner, mascara, and a touch of rouge on her cheeks and was surprised she remembered how to do it properly. It was so long ago since the last time she'd bothered with makeup. Her hair swept over her shoulders like fine silk.

Soledad liked the woman she saw in the mirror. She couldn't remember the last time she'd spent more than fifteen minutes on herself. Her idea of sprucing was a quick hop in the shower, gathering wet hair into a ponytail and shrugging into a T-shirt, and faded jeans.

Soledad liked too much what she saw, and her guilty conscience quickly took hold of her. She went to the bathroom, washed off the makeup, and bound her hair into a loose ponytail. Sprucing herself up when Elliot wasn't with her wasn't the message to telegraph.

Men were simple creatures. Their hormones were easily stirred by a look, a bit of cleavage, or a simple smile. Soledad didn't want to be responsible for triggering Carlo Moretti's hormones.

Did she? Soledad looked for the answer in the blue eyes coming at her from the mirror. No, she didn't want to stir Carlo Moretti's hormones. She wanted to awaken hers. She didn't dress up and make herself look good for a man she'd just met. She did it for herself.

The idea of adventure was a titillating concept. Besides, being married didn't signal death. She was a living, breathing woman with an appreciation for a man's eyes, and that was all she was interested in.

Eyeing herself in the mirror, Soledad loosened a few tendrils and let them flow around her face for a touch of glamour, not sexy. Not sexy, she told herself, twisting and turning in front of the dresser mirror.

It had been so long since she'd felt feminine and pretty, and it felt good.

Soledad heard her daughters' voices in her head.

"It never hurts to keep your man on his toes, Mom, and last I checked, Dad was a man." Those words of wisdom came with a wink from Hope.

"If it makes you feel good about yourself and gives you confidence, do it, Mom. It's about you. It should always be about you," Jasmine said.

"There's nothing wrong with making yourself look like a yummy-mummy," Annie and Allie simultaneously said with a snorted giggle.

They'd all be right, Soledad decided. She was doing it for herself.

Guilt tamped somewhat, Soledad dabbed perfume on her neck, wrists, and cleavage. She'd long forgotten what it was to concentrate on herself.

For too long, her life had centred on the children, Elliot, and home. As rewarding as it was, it led to a life that cascaded from one worry to the next, putting their lives in front of hers.

Soledad's guilt circled back, and her thoughts drifted to her family, and she stopped primping. "Christ, what am I doing? I'm a mother of four girls who look to me as their role model and a boy verging on manhood."

The twins, at seventeen, were at an impressionable age, as was Noah. Soledad's actions would impress on Noah's perception of the women in his life, his sisters, his first love, future girlfriends, his future wife, and Soledad.

Cynicism would supplant Noah's trust in the women in his life.

Conflicting emotions battered Soledad. She needed alcohol.

Soledad reached into the mini-fridge under the pantry, picked up the half-empty bottle of rum, uncapped it, and poured two fingers into a glass. The sizable, numbing gulp she took burned straight down to the sickness in her belly.

"Jesus, Soledad, you're not marrying the man. You're helping him with a pig roast." Soledad debated with herself as she paced the room. "Try to convince yourself of that when you've spent an hour getting ready."

Walking to the sliding doors, Soledad threw them open. The blast of tropical heat hit her like on her. Stepping onto the balcony, she breathed in the smell of roasting pig, sea brine, and perfume, floral and strong, from the manicured gardens. She stood gazing at the bold, bright colours of nature's beauty before her.

The high summer sun sparkled diamonds over teal waters that deepened in colour on the horizon and melded with the sky's blue. From the speakers set up throughout the beach as a beacon for the guests, Luis Fonsi seduced the *señoritas*. Skimpily clad bodies sheened on loungers around the massive kidney-shaped pool and beach. Screeching gulls flitted through the air, and vibrant coloured birds perched on palm trees joined in birdsong.

At the knock on the door, Soledad tossed part of her drink back and crossed to open it.

The glow of delight was swift on Carlo's face when he saw her. "Hello."

Soledad stood in the open door, looking at him. He smelled of chlorinated pool water, and his hair was curling with dampness on his neck. His wet T-shirt clung tight to his broad shoulders and solid chest. She couldn't take her eyes off him.

"Excuse my appearance, but I've come straight from my morning laps in the pool. I like to keep fit."

"Yes, you do." Soledad knocked the rest of the drink in her glass back to loosen the spear of lust and fire he drove to her belly. It marginally helped. "What are you doing here, Mr. Morelli?"

He nestled the dark lens sunglasses in the hair that hung in wet ropes and met the crystal blue eyes. "Are you going to invite me in?"

"No." Soledad moved to close the door, but he blocked it with his foot, immediately regretting the move. Flip-flops weren't the best footgear for blocking a door shut. "Just because you own this place doesn't mean you can invade my privacy," she said but left the door open when she walked to the pantry to top her glass of more liquid courage.

"If I recall, I knocked on your door, and you opened it. I did not use my master key to let myself in," he said, inviting himself into her room and closing the door behind him.

"Leave that open, please. We wouldn't want you to get the wrong impression. I'm a married woman."

Carlo propped the door open with his flip-flop. "You look great, by the way."

Soledad softened for a brief ten seconds before forcing herself to regain her composure. A display of weakness on a man like Carlo fed his ego. "I don't," she snapped.

"But you do." Carlo stepped forward and reached for the tucked strand of hair to let it fall loose. "It looks better that way." He found the flush that rose to her cheeks attractive.

Soledad tucked the strand back behind her ear. "What do you want, Mr. Moretti?"

Bemused eyebrows raised when he heard the formal address. He liked the spark in a woman. "I came to talk you into coming to the luau, but I see you had planned to do so already. Was it because I would be there?"

"No." Her swift, terse response elicited a dimpled smile from Carlo. As obvious in her disinterest, as she appeared to be, Carlo knew better. "Wipe that off your face. The smell of roasting pig made me hungry. It's the only reason I was considering joining the luau."

"Then, let's get you some of that roasting pig."

The warm glow he put in the pit of her stomach made her reconsider. "I've changed my mind. I won't be joining…." Soledad lost her train of thought when he came closer to her. "Umm … the …"

"Luau," Caro finished for her when she got a blank look on her face.

"Yeah, that."

Carlo slid his fingers under her chin and turned her face slowly to meet her eyes. "Do I make you nervous, Soledad?"

"No," she said, absently nodding.

"I do not mean to."

Soledad narked a safe distance between them. "This is all very awkward for me. I've never been alone without my husband by my side."

"You cannot think for yourself?"

Soledad set the glass on the round table. "You're young and unattached and can't understand the commitment shared between two people who've been married as long as Elliot and I have."

"I understand that you are here on your own." He crossed his arms and leaned a shoulder against the wall. "Why are you here, alone, Soledad? What do you hope to find here?"

Soledad held her glass in both hands and quietly stared at the golden liquid for a moment. "I ... I'm not sure."

"Well, whatever it is, I will help you find it." Carlo lay a hand over hers. It felt warm and real, and she yanked her hand away. "You do not need to feel nervous."

"I've never had another man's attention or touch on me. It doesn't seem right."

Carlo met her eyes. "I mean no disrespect by it. It is simply the appreciation of a man for a beautiful woman. You are meant to enjoy it."

"I'm old enough to be...."

"A beautiful, sexy woman."

Soledad snapped her head back. "Oh, I certainly am not that."

"I think you are." Carlo traced the curve of her cheek with his finger, and Soledad's shoulders tensed up. "And I mean to show you a good time while you are here. That is all."

Oh, Jesus. "A good time?"

"Drinks, dinner, and whatever may follow." Carlo reached for her hand, brought the palm to his mouth, and kissed it.

Sweet and sour Jesus, she thought when the deep, penetrating warmth made her pulse leap and gallop.

"You know what I would like to do now?"

Soledad's heart-pounding, she spun back, ready to refute whatever Carlo was prepared to offer.

"Get us both some of that roasted pig. That smell is contagious," he said.

She said, "I think you mean infectious."

"Yes, that does sound better." His lips curved.

On a laugh, the guilt that wrapped around her throat and choked her was replaced with anticipation. A woman who'd experienced little excitement, Soledad was ready for some.

Chapter 10

NOAH EASILY ACCESSED Soledad's bank accounts and Mastercard statement since she never changed the passwords after setting them up. Old people, Noah thought as he dove into an in-depth check of the transactions in both accounts.

Noah turned up no leads. The sharp fear that flooded Elliot grew into full panic mode. The tears wanted to come at the thought Soledad was lost to him. If he didn't know it before, he knew now that Soledad completed him, and he couldn't live without her.

Elliot's mind raced. The noise in his head made Elliot pause in the act of reaching for the coffee cup, and he rose to make his way to the bottle of Johnnie Walker on the credenza.

The study was filled with light glowing through the picture window as morning spread. The leaves on the linden tree in the front yard showed the rust, gold, and copper of the incoming season. As he liked, the front stretch of lawn was a lush green and mowed at a three-inch level plane. Soledad always kept an immaculate home for Elliot and the children, one they could be proud of.

Pouring two fingers, Elliot sent the whiskey streaming down his throat to settle his nerves and caught the collection of family photos. Every silver frame was angled at forty-five degrees on the polished credenza top. Elliot looked at the photos of Jasmine, Hope, Annie, Allie, and Noah at various stages of their life, but it was the one of Soledad and him on their wedding day that caught his eye.

Picking up the photo, he stared at it. Soledad looked angelic in the white, flowing gown. She held a cascading bouquet of white calla lilies and red roses. Her hair was a silk chestnut in contrast to the white lace veil that draped around her face. Her big crystal-blue eyes were full of love for him, as were his for her.

They were so young, so idealistic, and full of dreams. Soledad was nineteen and Elliot twenty-three when they found out she was pregnant, but so much in love, were they that marriage seemed the right decision.

Elliot and Soledad were married in a low-key ceremony with a handful of family only in attendance. The elaborate wedding of his mother's dream for her only child wouldn't happen because Elliot's father wouldn't permit it. Charles Winston Thomas wouldn't broadcast that the successor to his company had recklessly impregnated a young, naïve girl—not of his choosing—and had to marry in a shotgun wedding.

"Christ, Elliot, how's anyone to look up to me when I can't control what goes on in my own home? How's anyone to look up to you and respect you as a leader when you can't keep it in your pants and get a common girl pregnant? Because common she is, although not stupid. I'll give her that. She had you in her sights all along. This was her plan all along, and here you are, about to become a father and her personal ATM. Can't you see that?" Charles Winston Thomas barked in his imperious tone.

Charles would never let Elliot forget his mistake, nor would he welcome Soledad as a part of the family. A man desperate for his father's validation since marriage, Elliot allowed Charles to dismiss Soledad as someone unworthy of the Thomas name.

Elliot's mistakes were piling up, and he dropped his gaze to the photograph. "I'm sorry, Soledad. I'm sorry for letting you down." He set the photo down at exactly a forty-five-degree angle.

Elliot refilled the glass with three fingers of whiskey as Buddy strolled into the study. Sensing Elliot's distress, Buddy followed him to the desk and rested his head on his lap when he sat on the high-backed chair.

"If only you could talk. You know and hear everything around here," Elliot said, and the dog barked in agreement. "I have to find her, Buddy. I miss Soledad, and I need to make amends and ask for forgiveness. I need to say all the things I should have said when she was here. I need to wish her a happy birthday." His comment led him to think of candles and Soledad's utility drawer where she kept them.

Bolting to his feet, Elliot headed to the kitchen to rummage through the drawer Soledad used to store miscellaneous items. Maybe, he'd find something that led him to her.

Elliot found a stack of the month's receipts, which she'd use to cross-reference with the Mastercard statement. She had never seen a misreported charge in all the years of crosschecking, but consistency was key to excellence. That's what he told her like a mantra.

Elliot found warranties for appliances and electronics. Soledad was as organized as he'd demanded. He found pens and two marketing notepads from the local real estate agent. There were elastic bands and twist ties that Soledad couldn't bring herself to chuck in the garbage, but nothing useful to Elliot.

Coming up empty, Elliot walked back to the office and went through the desk again. Nothing.

Dashing to the bedroom, Elliot rummaged through Soledad's night table drawers, the closet, and the dresser. Nothing, and he found nothing that disclosed her whereabouts. Out of desperation, Elliot went through the medicine cabinet and was glad when he didn't see the drugs he imagined he would.

With Buddy in tow, Elliot went through every nook and cranny of the house, hoping to unearth anything that would lead him to Soledad. Zero. Nil. Zilch.

Soledad had disappeared off the face of the earth.

Panic began to bubble in Elliot's throat.

What if he never found her? What if she never came back? The what-ifs rolling ceaselessly in his head, Elliot reached into his pants pocket for his phone. He called Hope and Jasmine. However calm Elliot's voice was during the video call to his daughters, a wave of nausea swept through him the entire time. Neither Hope nor Jasmine had seen or spoken to Soledad in a couple of days.

Elliot called Christine next. Her voice mail informed the caller she was in the Congo for the next two months and would call back when possible.

Elliot discounted Soledad running off to the Congo to be with her sister because only Christine did crazy. As much as Elliot didn't entertain Noah's comment that no one in their right mind volunteered to hang out in the Congo, he had to agree with his son.

Elliot thought hard of whom to call next and came up empty. Aside from her sister, Soledad's list of friends was nonexistent. Soledad had no one to talk to or turn to, and that was on him.

He'd never liked nor approved of Soledad's friends and never made an effort to get to know them. Soledad distanced herself from them in time, and that was also on him. His thoughtless, inconsiderate, and lack of interest in her life drove her to desperate measures.

Guilt, remorse, fear, and shock washed over Elliot at once. He felt the emptiness, and the sense of permanent loss loomed in his mind.

It was time to do what he didn't want to, but desperate times called for desperate measures. Elliot pulled out his phone, dialled nine-one-one, and hoped it wouldn't get back to his father.

Chapter 11

SOMETIMES, YOU NEED to check your mind out of the moment for your sanity, and Soledad did that.

Outside, in the raw hot air and the festive party atmosphere, Soledad forgot her life. For a few hours, Soledad fell into the dream that was Topaz Island.

Soulful music thrummed merrily from speakers scattered on the beach. Servers in floral shirts and white pants or skirts passed fruity drinks with tiny umbrellas to guests. Long tables covered in white linen overflowed with a selection of spicy island foods. The air was ripe with good, rich ocean and grilled fish scents. Weed was passed around like candy at Halloween. People milled about, talked, drank, and danced where the mood struck.

Soledad was in the midst of it and loved every minute.

Soledad couldn't remember having this much fun. In between the fun, Soledad drank piña coladas—now her favourite drink. Her fourth piña colada awakened the adventurous woman in her, and every inhibition that had held her back vanished.

The extrovert Soledad she'd stifled for too long was a fun woman who enjoyed dancing, drinking, laughing, and smoked weed when the spliff came her way. The freedom to do as she wanted without looking over her shoulder or adhering to the conventions expected of a wife and mother of five felt liberating.

He'd watched her all afternoon as he did then. Carlo's lips twitched as Soledad attempted to conga. He appreciated her flexibility. Any man would. And they would let their mind conjure the fantasies that crossed his mind then and put an appreciative smile on his face. There was nothing like a flexible woman to whet a man's interest.

When Soledad fell back onto the sand, Carlo's instinct was to rush to check on her, but he held back when she burst out laughing and moved to make sand angels. Before he knew it, Soledad had everyone joining in.

The Soledad before him wasn't the tense, nervous woman he met on the tarmac last night. Grant it, alcohol spurred the real Soledad to break from her cocoon, but it nonetheless pleased Carlo to see her capitulate to her true self.

"May I help you up?" Carlo stepped up beside her and put out his hand.

"Don't you want to make a sand angel?" Her blue eyes twinkled with fun.

"Thank you, but I like sand on the ground, not inside me. Now, let us get some coffee in you."

"I don't think so." Soledad took the offered hand and bounced to her feet. "It'll kill this great buzz I have going."

"That is the point for the coffee."

"Do you know how well the combination of piña coladas," she essed for emphasis, "doobie," her voice dropped to a whisper, "feels like?"

"I will confess I do, and I will admit it is a good feeling."

"Then why do you want to kill it?"

"Because you are slurring your words." Carlo waved Mariela over and asked her to bring a strong pot of coffee.

"Buzz killer. Now you sound like my husband." Soledad smoothed her hair and skirt with slow, uncoordinated movements.

"Are you all right?" Carlo asked when a crown of uneasiness creased her face.

"I see what you mean about wanting the sand to remain on the ground." She twisted her body right, left trying to shake the sand from places it shouldn't be, and Carlo flashed that smile that liquefies a woman's insides. Her insides nearly evaporated.

"Let us get you into a sitting position." Carlo walked Soledad to the closest lounge chair and helped her down when she nearly missed her landing.

Lying flat on her back on the lounge chair, Soledad peeled her eyes to a sky painted like a forest fire as the sun set for the day. Over the sound of bass guitars and bongos from the romantic bachata flowing, Soledad heard the sound of the roiling ocean waves rolling in and pulling back.

Soledad thought of Elliot then and wondered what he'd think if he saw her now.

Elliot was a good husband and provider. He was her best friend. He loved the children, and although he didn't express it physically or said it anymore, Soledad knew he loved her. Soledad only wished he didn't take life so seriously.

Elliot didn't drink or smoke. That wasn't a bad thing, but occasionally you need to let your hair down and let loose. Everyone needs an escape from the demands of everyday life, to do the unordinary for a few hours to unwind.

Elliot would rather spend his nights locked up in his office than go to dinner, and God forbid he'd consider spending a few hours at a bar just the two of them or go to a concert or their neighbour's pool party.

Soledad imagined the twisted look on Elliot's face if he saw her sprawled on a lounge chair in front of hundreds of people, her head swimming with alcohol and weed. She let out a loud snort of laughter.

"You are having a good time?" Carlo sat at the edge of her chair and breathed the air scented with her perfume.

"I am. I so am."

He fell into the comfortable silence with her. There was much to be said for not needing to make endless, empty conversation for the sake of companionship.

"It's so beautiful here," Soledad said after some time had passed.

Casually, Carlo wound a strand of her hair around his finger. "As are you."

Soledad braced herself on her elbows. The diamond on her finger sparkled brightly. Carlo disregarded it. "Do you really believe that, or are you saying it to get me into bed?" she asked with brazen alcohol-induced confidence.

"I will not deny I would love to get you into bed, but I do not say what I do not mean. You are beautiful, Soledad." He loosened her hair and let it spill around her face.

"You can have any woman here you want, and there are loads of gorgeous, fit, tight bodies here. Why me? I'm a middle-aged … nearly middle-aged woman," she corrected.

"You are middle-aged."

Her eyes changed, sobered. "Well, thank you for that."

"Not by sight. I have access to the guest's records, remember."

She massaged her temples to ward away the massive headache coming on. "Right. Do the records tell you that I'm at the point where things I didn't know could sag." When Soledad shook her head to dismiss the image of her naked body that popped into her head, she felt the effects of too many piña coladas. "Oh, Jesus," she mumbled, rubbing her temples in a circular motion.

"That right there is why." Carlo reached for the cup of black coffee Mariela had left on the table and held it out for her.

Soledad took the cup and sipped coffee. "What do you mean by that right there is why?"

"Aside from the fact that you are beautiful, you are not obvious or using your feminine wiles to get my attention. In my book, that vulnerability and honesty are very attractive. Are you very religious, Soledad?"

The question took her for a loop. "Why do you ask?"

"I hear you say His name," Carlo pointed upward, "often as if in prayer." Soledad snorted a laugh. "Would you like to go for a walk on the beach? It will help shake the sand from wherever it is hiding."

"Okay," she said, fearful of how quickly she gave in and how much she wanted to. "Where are we going?"

Carlo took the coffee cup in Soledad's hands. "It is a surprise."

Carlo led her away from the lit area into the moonlit part of the beach. Guided by the moonlight, they followed the curve of the beach. The air smelled of salt carried by the ocean plunged in black.

They reached the pier that marked the end of Carlo's property a mile later.

"That is home for me." Carlo's eyes flicked to the impressive sleek, racing yacht anchored at the end of the pier.

"That's impressive," she said of the one-hundred-foot boat swaying in tune to the ocean water that crashed against the length of its hull. The sails were down, and strings of multi-coloured lights twinkled brightly against the dark in their place. "You live on it?"

Nodding, Carlo took her hand and led her to the end of the pier. "I am at the resort for most of the day, entertaining, dealing with the staff and issues. By nightfall, I must disconnect, and this is where I come to do so. It has all the comforts of the resort plus solitude because sometimes you would like to be alone with a pretty lady." He boarded the boat and gave her his hand. "Would you like to board The Xanadu?" Carlo watched Soledad gnaw her bottom lip as she debated. "Sometimes, Soledad, the unknown is better than the known. What do you say?"

Chapter 12

Twenty-Four Hours Later

"I LIKE TO report a missing person. Yes, fine, I'll speak to whomever you want me to." Elliot regretted the curt tone, but he didn't have the patience to be bounced from desk to desk.

Phone pressed to his ear, Elliot stood at the bedroom window. The day had flown by, and daylight had given way to night without realizing it. Elliot watched the gleaming eyes of a raccoon as he shuffled its way across the backyard and triggered the light motion sensor. Under the pool of light, Elliot could see the lemon yellow and apple red of fall crowning the trees Soledad had planted for each of their children at birth. Hope's was a lilac, Jasmine's was a red maple, the twins were tall firs, and Noah's a birch tree.

Soledad's pride and joy, the garden was transformed into a pageant of autumn hue. Orange, burgundy, and pink mums burst with colour, as did the calla lilies, marigolds, asters, and sweet alyssum. The grass, boxwood, and ferns were neatly trimmed. Neat and order with a touch of splendour was Soledad's way. Yet another of Soledad's endeavours that brought pleasure and pride into their lives he'd taken for granted.

Elliot's regrets were growing by the minute.

The pool was drained and covered for the incoming winter season. He wouldn't know where to begin on how to winterize the pool they'd installed after the twins came along as a means to entertain four high-spirited girls.

Elliot couldn't count the number of get-togethers and parties Soledad held for the girls, Noah, and him over the years. The boundless reserves of energy and patience it took to accomplish such a feat were monumental. Entertaining five children and the swarms of friends who tagged took the patience and energy he never possessed. But Soledad's devotion, that of a mother and wife, resulted in bright, well-mannered, well-adjusted, respectful, ambitious children and his career advancement.

Elliot's appreciation for Soledad had long gone overlooked. Elliot saw that now, but his focus was on financially sustaining the family. Soledad had never worked, and as the provider of six, the burden fell solely on Elliot's shoulders.

There were braces to think about, the latest laptops, cell phones, and clothes. Teenage girls could shop twenty-four-seven, and to his disappointment, Elliot found out boys could also. There was private school tuition for five children, which Elliot insisted on. Soledad wasn't a demanding woman and had told him public school was just as good, but Elliot had his standing in the company and something to prove to his father. Appearances had to be maintained.

It was why Elliot had to inherit his father's firm. Ownership of Thomas and Partners would allow Elliot to maintain his family in the lifestyle they had become accustomed to. At least that's what Elliot told himself because at the heart of it was proving he was as capable and accomplished a man as his father.

"Constable Watkins, how may I help you?" said the voice at the end of the line, and Elliot hung up.

His father couldn't know Soledad was gone. Elliot had to find Soledad himself. How and where was the question?

Chapter 13

"WOULD YOU LIKE to board The Xanadu?" Carlo repeated, meeting the confused blue eyes.

His alluring smile, one Soledad imagined he used with great effect to seduce women to his bed and keep them there, to her distress, was working on her. Soledad closed her fingers over her wedding band and thought of Elliot, Noah, and the girls. She thought of her wedding vows. *I will love and honor you all the days of my life* was what Soledad had promised to do on her wedding day, until death did them part.

Christ! What am I doing here?

Soledad was about to walk away when she made the mistake of looking Carlo in the eye. The yearning she saw in them was a look she hadn't seen in Elliot's in a long, long time. It made her feel wanted and feminine, desired. She hadn't felt that way in too long.

The inexplicable power of a man's coveting look clouded Soledad's mind and set her emotions in turmoil. Carlo would kindle the smothered flame in her and wouldn't starve the fire once lit.

You're a mother and a wife, Soledad. This isn't right. It isn't the example you want to set for the children. She warred between loyalty to her husband and family and herself.

Emotions, too many with mixed messages, slammed her and fogged her brain as it wandered to unforbidden thoughts.

The woman in her needed this wanted this. Soledad wanted the touch of a man who desired her, the eye of one who admired her. She wanted to feel the tug, the pull, the unabashed arousal that a man's touch induces. Soledad wanted to hear passionate, loving words whispered in her ear.

The tightening in her gut, raw and intense, made her conjure the thoughts that led to the liquid warmth to spread in her belly. She was too vulnerable, and Carlo was becoming a danger to her.

What was this man doing to her?

Soledad moved back, marking a safe distance between them. She needed to think. Should she board The Xanadu, or shouldn't she? Soledad thought and debated, mumbled to herself while Carlo silently watched her pace the pier.

Her mind snapping clear, Soledad decided to go back to the resort and head straight to her room.

As she turned to walk away, Carlo reached for her hand. "Don't go, Soledad."

Soledad took in a long slow breath and let it out slowly. The option to do the right or wrong thing is the only one you have.

Chapter 14

ELLIOT'S PHONE RANG.

He moved quickly to pull the phone out of his pants pocket. "Soledad, hello, hello, Soledad, is that you?" Elliot listened intently to the caller. He disconnected and tossed the phone on the table after listening to the recorded spam message for a few seconds. "Fucking trolls. Those people need to be hanged." Elliot ran a frustrated hand through his hair.

"Here they are, Dad." Noah walked into the kitchen with Annie and Allie trailing.

"Hey, Dad." Annie bent down and kissed Buddy's head when he rose to his feet and trotted to her side.

Allie followed with, "Is Mom back yet?"

Like her sister, Allie's streaked brown hair and straight-cut bangs fountained around the freckled sprinkled face, with cobalt eyes and a delicately upturned nose. Both sisters wore pink sweaters and black spandex leggings. They were tall and lithe, and although their interest in ballet lasted for two short years, the graceful movement of the ballet dancer remained ingrained in them.

The girls looked so much like Soledad, Elliot thought, staring at them. "Your mother is what I want to talk to the two of you about." Elliot lowered to the chair and took a moment before he said, "Your mother is … gone."

"We know that, but where is she?" Allie and Annie said in unison.

Elliot steadied himself with a long breath. "I don't know."

"But she's going to be back soon, right?" Allie sat across from her father.

"I hope so, 'cause I'm starving," Annie poked her head in the refrigerator, scanning its contents for something to eat.

"Me too," Allie echoed. "Get me the bag of baby carrots and the Ranch dip, Annie. I feel peckish."

"Jesus, you guys are stupid." Noah rolled his eyes to the sky. "Mom's gone."

"We know that dipshit. It's why we're asking." Annie tossed the bag of carrots to her sister, who tossed a couple to Buddy.

Elliot pressed fingers to his temple. "Guys, stop. Annie, sit down." He took a pause to line up his thoughts. "Your mother is gone, and I don't know where to."

Annie stopped mid-air from setting the dip container on the table when she saw the seriousness on her father's face. "What are you saying, Dad?" Annie asked, hoping for an answer that didn't match her thoughts.

"We all fucked up."

"What have I said about speaking that way, Noah?" Elliot said

"Well, we did, Dad. We all forgot her birthday. Her fiftieth, which seemed to be a big deal for Mom. She got pissed at all of us, and she skipped. Left. Disappeared." Noah tossed out with an impatient hiss at his dense sisters.

Allie stopped the carrot mid-way to her mouth. "Oh. Shit. We did. How could we forget, Annie?"

"All of us did, me included," Elliot said.

"Wait, what do you mean gone?" Annie stared at her weasel brother.

"We don't know where she is." Noah filled in his sisters on his computer search and on coming up empty.

"We need to call the cops." Annie's eyes brimmed with tears.

"Yeah, that's what we need to do, Dad." Allie wrapped a comforting arm around her sister's shoulder. "We need to find her."

"Don't worry, girls. I'll find her." Elliot assured his children.

"What if she doesn't want to be found, Dad?" Allie said with tears flowing from her eyes.

Elliot had no response.

Part II

The Middle

There are times when fantasy love is better than reality love.

— Andy Warhol

Chapter 15

Twenty-Five Hours Later

"JOIN ME ABOARD The Xanadu, Soledad. We will share a cup of coffee and cake under this beautiful star-filled sky. Coffee and cake," Carlo repeated in the easy way he had with women.

Coffee and cake, is that what they called it now?

Soledad stared at him. Behind the smile that held warmth and easy invitation, Soledad didn't need to transcribe the coded look in his eyes to understand the message.

She stood where she was, torn between staying and leaving.

Boarding the boat would splinter the vow she made to the man she loved and the promises she'd made to Elliot, and the lasting effect it would have on her children was immeasurable. It would setback the principles of trust, devotion, and fidelity she'd instilled in them. Cynicism would replace innocence, skepticism would replace trust, hurt, and anger would supplant love. Soledad wanted none of that to touch her children, and diluting her principled-ness wasn't an option.

But what about her happiness? She'd set it by the wayside for too long. The loneliness, discontent in her life, and the erosion of confidence in herself made her feel like a marginal woman. The demoralizing feeling had eaten away at her for too long and poisoned her heart and soul.

She wasn't getting any younger, and when would she catch the eye of a gorgeous, virile, thirty-two-year-old man again? And. And. And.

Soledad needed this, if only for one night. She considered her options, discarded them. One night, she told herself on a remote island where no one knew her wouldn't hurt anyone.

Without a word, Soledad held her hand out to Carlo. Taking her hand, he cupped it protectively and helped her embark The Xanadu.

"Welcome aboard The Xanadu, Soledad Thomas,"

There was no way back from the moment, only forward into an uncertain future of consequences.

Chapter 16

A MOON SLICED in half sat high in the sky. Its light sailed white over the brackish water. Soledad smelled the ocean's brine, pungent and strong, in the air. She heard the faint echo of Bob Marley's Three Little Birds flowing from the resort along with laughter.

Carlo walked Soledad starboard and gathered her close to him. When she felt his strong arms go around her, she held stiff for a moment. The warmth of his embrace radiated over her, and she melted in his arms, as he wanted her to.

Soledad had long forgotten what it felt like to be wrapped in the circle of a man's arms and be held, and she let herself fall into him.

Her head pillowed against his chest, they remained that way for a long while. In the stillness of the night, they listened to the rhythmic whoosh of ocean waves, and the ocean whisper.

After sharing a cup of coffee and delicious passion fruit and mango cake, Soledad felt relaxed and comfortable. Her doubtful mind and the guilt of whether she had made the right decision by boarding *The Xanadu* faded.

"I like your hair down, Soledad," he said, loosening her bound hair and letting it rain around her face down to her shoulders. "Are you nervous, Soledad?"

Soledad took a few steps in retreat. "I've never done this before." Carlo said nothing, merely stared at her standing by the railing looking out at the water. "There are rules when you're married," she said when she turned toward him.

Under the splash of moonlight as a warm breeze fluttered over her face, caressing her hair, he thought she looked like a siren that appeared from the depths of the water. Her face should be on canvass, hanging on museum walls to be appreciated.

Carlo walked toward her. "So I've heard, although I wouldn't know what they are. I've never been married."

"You're crowding me a bit."

Carlo's sexy, full lips curved into a smile. "You're very beautiful, Soledad."

"You exaggerate." Recognizing the look in Carlo's eyes, Soledad breathed in deep to balance herself from what was coming.

"I don't." Keeping his eyes on hers, he smiled that smile that liquefied her insides. "I want you, Soledad. I want you badly." Carlo brushed his fingers over her hair, down her cheek, to her chest.

Soledad felt her skin tingle beneath his touch. "Oh, Jesus!"

"I desire you, Soledad, more than I have any woman."

"Oh, Christ!" she repeatedly said, in between long, slow breaths to calm herself when he kissed her fingers one at a time.

"I want to kiss you, Soledad." His mouth a whisper from hers made Soledad's stomach muscles tighten. "Would you let me kiss you?"

Urge overpowering her restraint, to regain her control Soledad thought of the vows she'd made to Elliot before family and God. She thought of the life they'd built in a place that meant home to them. Soledad thought of her girls and Noah.

"No, you may not kiss me," she said, but her head nodded her acquiescence.

Carlo responded by tenderly brushing his lips to hers and lingering long enough to haze her head and derail every thought in it.

"I want to touch you and explore your body with my hands and mouth. Will you stay with me tonight?"

Chapter 17

ALLIE FLIPPED THE bedroom light on and closed the door at her back after Annie and Buddy walked in. Allie's room, unlike Annie's, was an oasis of calm and order. The walls were painted in a pastel purple tone, and the frilly bedspread on the button-tufted platform bed matched it. Lavender lace framed the picture window overlooking the garden and pool. Posters of Adele, Taylor Swift, and Beyoncé hung above her bed.

"Where do you think Mom went? Where do you think she is?" Allie fell onto the carpeted floor, and Buddy walked up and lay his head on her lap. "You miss Mom too, don't you, boy?" She scratched Buddy's head when his soulful eyes looked at her.

"I don't know, Allie. I'm not a mind reader." Annie sat next to her sister cross-legged with the laundry basket before her. "That's why I'm going through the laundry basket."

"Do you think she's coming back?" Emotion and fear choked Allie's voice.

"I don't know, but I sure as hell hope so." Annie fished her way through the neatly folded clothes in the laundry basket. "I can't make it through one day without Mom. Who's going to cook our meals? The best I can do is fry eggs, and I can't live on eggs alone."

"So typical of you to think only about yourself." Allie began to sob. "What if she doesn't want to come back?"

"Control yourself, Allie. You too, Buddy." Annie ordered when Buddy, sensing Allie's sadness, began to whimper. "Hopefully, we'll find Mom's cell in this laundry and find something on it. Et voilà." Annie held the phone up when she found it underneath the towels. "Pfft, idiot techie brother thinks he knows all. It would've never dawned on him to check for Mom's phone in the laundry basket. Stop whimpering, Allie, and make yourself useful. Plug it in to charge."

Allie wiped at tears with her hands and did as her bossy older sister—by one minute—said. "It would have never dawned on Dad either, but then neither has been forced by Mom to put clean their clothes away."

"True that." Annie tapped on the phone's screen when it bloomed to life and scrolled through the call history.

"Check WhatsApp. I recently installed it for her so she can talk to Aunt Christine."

"Hmmm, maybe that's where she's stashed the contact info for the boy-toy she's hiding from us."

"That's not funny, Annie, and keep your voice down. You don't want to put ideas into Dad's head. He's freaked out enough as is." Allie absently stroked Buddy's head as he snored into the doggie dream.

"I'm sure the thought has already crossed Dad's mind. Mom's turning fifty, and I've read that old people go through this midlife crunch that makes them do crazy things like buying expensive sports cars or get a younger squeeze."

"I think you mean mid-life crises, and Mom's not after a younger squeeze."

"Whatever, and you keep telling yourself whatever makes you feel good. Nope, the only calls and texts are to Aunt Christine, Jasmine, Hope, Noah, Dad, and us. There are some to Buddy's dog groomer, to the pharmacy, and one to Swift Lube. In the words of Gordon Ramsay, fucking hell, Mom doesn't have a life, does she?"

"Is that language necessary, Annie?" Allie barked.

"Pardon me, Mother Teresa."

"And no, Mom has no life outside of us, but we're supposed to be her life."

Annie's eyebrows winged up. Her sister could be so simple-minded sometimes. "Mom needs more than us. She needs to feel like a woman, even if she is old. She needs...." Annie stopped short of saying a man's eyes and touch, something she hadn't seen their father do in forever. Allie wasn't as liberal thinking as Annie was and wouldn't be receptive to the remark.

"You're thinking Mom needs Dad in ... that way."

Annie snorted a laugh when Allie winced. "Yes, Allie. Mom may be old, but she's not dead. "When was the last time you heard Mom and Dad ... you know, going at it."

"Shit, Annie, did you need to put that goddamn thought in my head?"

The smirk twisted Annie's lips. "Shocking language, Mother Teresa."

"Oh, shut the fuck up." Allie snapped, waking Buddy from his doggie slumber. "Sorry, Buddy, go back to sleep."

"I wouldn't put it past Mom if she had a gorgeous boy-toy somewhere. You know Mom's still a looker when she bothers to fix herself up. At least that's what I've heard Noah's friends say."

The comment set Allie's mind racing. "Stop it. You're wrong. She would never do that. And major yuck on Noah's friends eyeing mom."

"All I know is I'd get super tired, not to mention bored out of my mind staying home all day. Imagine your day-to-day focus being only your family, laundry, shopping, picking up prescriptions, and all the housewife bullshit that comes when you don't have a career. I'd die if that became my life. I have to pee." Annie rose and walked around Allie and Buddy happily snoring again.

Allie's thoughtful eyes followed Annie to the bathroom. "You're different than Mom. She loves domestic life and likes to take care of us and our home."

"Sure, you tell yourself that," Annie said over the sound of flushing water. "Mom's still a woman." She soaped her hands and ran them under warm water.

"And?"

Allie might be the smarter of the two, but she lacked female thinking skills, Annie thought. "Like I said, it's been ages since I heard Mom and Dad getting busy, and when was the last time you remember Dad taking her for a romantic dinner, just the two of them. Do you remember them going on a trip without any of us?"

Allie got the worry line between her eyebrows. "Never."

"My point."

"But dad is busy working to earn a living to support us. Mom should understand that."

"Working hard to get the needed validation from grandad is what you mean. It's one thing for us to forget Mom's birthday. It's another for Dad to do so after dismissing her all these years."

Instant distress ran across Allie's face. "Do you really think she's got someone on the side and that he's swooped her away all because Daddy forgot her birthday?"

"All I'm saying is I wouldn't blame her if she wanted some attention to make her feel desirable and like a wanted woman."

"What do you know about feeling like a wanted woman? You're seventeen." Allie scoffed.

"So are you, Miss I'll-laugh-at-any-insipid-thing, Jerry Stottlemeyer says. If that doesn't scream, 'I want attention,' I don't know what does."

"Fine. Yes. I get the point." The worry line between Allie's eyebrows formed deeper. "And thanks for putting the thought of Mom with a boy toy into my head."

"Just saying." Annie picked up the cell phone off the bed. "I'm going to let dad know I found her phone and that there's nothing on it."

"Wait, maybe we should be looking for a burner phone." Allie's comment caused Annie to raise dramatic brows. "What? Mom watches TV. Maybe she has one to communicate with ah, Jesus, I can't believe I'm saying this, her boy-toy." Allie didn't like the sound of that, but this was now their reality.

Chapter 18

SOLEDAD'S HEAD WAS still swimming under the effects of luau piña coladas, but there was no misreading what she saw in Carlo's eyes. Soledad saw everything she yearned for in them, adventure and excitement, fire and romance. She thought about that for a moment and concluded she couldn't buck the responsible woman in her to scratch the needy woman's itch.

At Soledad's hesitation, Carlo walked to her and brushed back the hair that danced around her face. Looking into her big blue puzzled eyes glided his lips over hers. In one instant, she became intimate with the taste and texture of his tongue. The kiss made every bone in her body go limp, and she softened under him—just a little.

Soledad stared at Carlo as if she'd never seen him or anything quite like him. "Mr. Morelli, you take liberties," she retorted to mask the quick, deep penetrating warmth his kiss unleashed inside her.

"I will admit I have, but I could not resist it anymore, Soledad. Since the first night I saw you, I felt a connection with you and have wanted to kiss you."

"Well, don't. You forget I'm a married woman," she said, but there was no resentment, remorse, or anger in Soledad's voice, only the sound of retrospection.

She liked Carlo's kiss and the feelings he'd stirred in her that made her feel wanted. The lingering satisfaction eased the tension from Soledad's shoulders and shut down the storm of indecision warring in her head.

Soledad felt no regret when she reached for his hand and allowed him to lead her below deck.

Warm tones, beige, and brown were the theme throughout his cabin. The floor was teak, polished to a shine. A king-size bed covered in cream silk sat atop a platform. There were glossy, oak night tables on either side of the bed and a bench covered in buttery-soft leather at its feet. There was a sitting area facing a large screen television embedded in the wall. Windows ran the room's length and stared out to an ocean misted in a haze of blue.

Soledad watched Carlo walk around the room, lighting the dozens of lavender-scented candles while Norah Jones passionately asked to come away with her.

When Carlo reached for her hand to walk her to the bed, Soledad's stomach pitched and rolled. What if she didn't meet his expectations? What if he was expecting a Mrs. Robinson-like moment from her? He had to be expecting experience and skill from a married woman, and she possessed neither. If there was one thing marital sex guaranteed, it was repetition and monotony.

She watched television. She saw what young couples did in the bedroom. Christ! She could never contort her body that way. Worse, what if her fifty-year-old body repulsed him? Most days, it sickened her. The sagging and bulging were too much for anyone to deal with. She couldn't allow him to see her naked. No way, no how.

Rattled by the thought, Soledad shook her head. "I can't do this." She turned to leave.

He reached for her hand and pulled her to him. "Do not be afraid, Soledad." Carlo's unforeseen next move surprised her and made her heart burst like flowers in spring.

Taking her in his arms, Carlo circled the room with her in a slow seductive dance. The warmth that came over her ignited the female light long extinguished.

Nora Jones segued into Luther Vandross's *Here and Now*, and Carlo sang along. Carlo's voice flowing musically with Luther's, he spun Soledad around the room and melted her heart as he did.

"How did you know Luther is one of my favourite singers?"

"I did not know. What I do know is that Luther can win any woman over."

"Is that what you're trying to do? Win me over to become a notch on your bedpost."

Carlo pulled back far enough to see her eyes. "Never think of yourself in those terms. Never, you hear me?" At his firm stare, Soledad nodded.

Gathering her back in, Carlo clung tightly to her and picked up where he left off with Luther and sang. "*You're more than I dare to dream. I need you.*"

With the soft music drifting and the ocean splashing against the boat, Soledad pressed her face to his chest, closed her eyes, and let Carlo take her away into the romantic, dreamlike moment.

Steering her toward the bed, Carlo laid her back. "*I look in your eyes, and there I see what happiness really means.*" His voice flowed with Luther's in harmony.

Sex had never been a driving force in her life, but it was what Soledad wanted tonight. Soledad wanted her blood to flame, her skin to sear under his touch. She wanted the heat to hit her like a punch to the stomach.

Soledad wanted to give herself to Carlo, and she wanted his hands over her body.

Honour required difficulty. Honour and moral rectitude be damned, she thought and cupping an arm behind his head, she pulled Carlo in and covered his mouth with hers. The skilled slide of her tongue was drugging and potent. Emotions, need, want, and desire, stirred and surged to the surface and she poured them into the kiss.

His lips still tingling, Carlo's face lit like the sun. "I like that, Soledad Thomas." He played his mouth over hers. "I like that very much."

Carlo's lips trailed down to her neck. Hands gliding over her shoulders, he tugged at the thin straps, and she moved to stop him.

She wanted this, wanted him, but it was so long since she'd had anyone's eyes but Elliot's rove her naked body. And it had been a long while since Elliot had done any roving. What would Carlo think of her nude body? What would he think?

"I … I don't feel comfortable with…." Soledad left the sentence hanging. How did she tell him her confidence in her appearance was nonexistent?

"I would like to see you, all of you," he murmured, tugging the dress away.

The glow of delight on Carlo's face was swift when he saw the white lace bra and panties. He eased back to take her in a while, expressing his pleasure in the Italian words he murmured as he gaped at her.

"I don't understand what any of that means, and not that I need to because it all sounded amazing. I just hope they're words of approval."

He smiled suddenly. "They most certainly are, Soledad. You are *bellissima*." His fingers ran down the swells of her breasts over the soft flesh above the lace of her bra. "That translates into very beautiful." A quick surge of confidence replaced nerves and panic, and Soledad's rigid body loosened. "Yes, Soledad, relax and enjoy my touch." Carlo leaned in and glided his lips over the swells of her breasts, nipping at the nipples straining against lace.

The quiet, throaty moans she made shot a spear of heat to his loins, and she felt him go hard. Nothing made a woman feel more feminine than to have a man show his appreciation and stare at her as if he'd been bewitched.

She had the power now, and it felt glorious.

"I want you, Soledad. I want you so much it hurts. I want to make love with you all night long. I want to be inside you and feel you close to me," Carlo murmured with hunger and desire.

With the feeling of feminine power coiled inside her, Soledad pushed his shirt off his shoulders to dig into warm flesh and trace the hard body.

Tonight her life would be filled with a wonderful peace, she thought.

SOLEDAD DIDN'T FEEL LIKE A PASSING ship in the night or a notch on Carlo's bedpost. Carlo made her feel desired and fueled her ego, not his. That was how she felt each time he turned to her with a ravenous look in his eyes.

He wanted her, fifty-year-old her and meant it.

Carlo had told her she was beautiful when his hands skimmed her body. His eyes were filled with admiration and want when he explored her body. Looking at her in the way he did, fueled her femininity and confidence.

Carlo had awakened her and kindled needs Soledad hadn't felt in so long. He was patient and guided her when needed without judgement. And she'd needed a lot of guidance. Carlo showed her nuances in lovemaking she knew nothing about and hadn't ridiculed, shamed, or embarrassed her when she faltered. He didn't judge the naiveté of an older married woman who should know better.

His eyes were full of need when he was inside her, and when he filled her, he cried out her name like a melody as he powered the shocking waves of pleasure through her.

The man couldn't have made the moment more perfect if she'd concocted it in her head.

Love had been enough for Soledad, the mother and wife, but Carlo showed her it hadn't been enough. The woman in her wanted to be touched as Carlo had. She wanted to feel naughty, wanted, and appreciated as Carlo made her feel.

In the aftermath of their lovemaking, wrapped in the comfort of Carlo's arms, they watched the dawn of a new day as a dark sky transformed into a dreamy blue.

Soledad was hard-pressed to remember the last time she and Elliot had watched the sunrise after making love. Familiarity erodes intimacy, spontaneity, and romance in a couple.

"Are you hungry, Soledad? I can make you breakfast." Carlo reached for Soledad's hand and linked his fingers with hers.

Soledad's eyes darted from the window to Carlo. "Let's stay like this for a while. Do you mind?"

"I do not." He lifted her hand and pressed it to his mouth. "If that is what you want, that is what we will do. But if you are up to it, I will be ready to go in another, oh, fifteen minutes."

Smiling eyes looked at him—the wonder of youth.

Chapter 19

ELLIOT'S TIRED MIND journeyed to places he never thought he would.

Was Soledad with another man? If she was, how long had it been going on? Was it going on right under his roof, in his children's home, in their bed?

Elliot formed opinions about a woman he realized he didn't know anymore.

A man had to be at the heart of Soledad's decision to disappear. Why else would a married woman, a mother of five, leave her family without saying a word? Why would Soledad betray him?

She'd been acting strangely for months, but he attributed it to boredom. With Hope and Jasmine out of the house, the twins, and Noah living independent lives, being at home all day, alone, without much to do, had to get tedious.

While working his fingers to the bone for her and the family, Soledad was— Elliot couldn't bring himself to think about what Soledad was doing.

With a sigh, Elliot told himself he needed to focus.

His mind calmer, Elliot questioned his role in Soledad's disappearance. It took two to create a situation. Had he driven her into the arms of another man because of his lack of actions and words? But after a lifetime together, Soledad shouldn't need words or actions. They were unspoken words and actions that should be understood between two people who'd shared a bed for years.

He hadn't said it for a long time, but he loved Soledad and always would. She should know that. She was the mother of his five children, for God's sake.

Elliot hadn't told her how much he appreciated her, but he did. He hadn't done much for Soledad lately, and he hadn't said the words she needed to hear. He admitted it to himself, but he shouldn't have to. It was an understood sentiment between couples who'd shared a lifetime, five children, and a dog.

That was the sum of him.

Taking the last of his coffee, Elliot decided he needed to shower off the last few hours of the most difficult day of his life.

SOLEDAD FELT LIKE A RENEWED WOMAN.

In bed, snuggled in Carlo's arms, they talked about everything and nothing. The boat swayed under the steady whoosh of waves. Beyond the cabin window, the bold morning sun rained over the vast blue ocean. A seagull effortlessly glided in the air before diving into the water, snaping breakfast, and surfacing with the fish in its beak.

Soledad was having a secret, passionate love affair with a man who talked to her and found her sexy. Having a man, this man's complete attention and hunger for her added the irresistible element of excitement Soledad lacked. Carlo changed how she perceived herself.

She wanted the euphoric feeling to stay with her forever.

That was the sum of her.

Chapter 20

SOLEDAD AND CARLO made love in the shower and not your run-of-the-mill sex under the spray of hot water. Sticky, sweet-tasting honey, addictive chocolate syrup, and nuts were used as props. Never in Soledad's wildest dream would she have thought to use either of those ingredients outside the kitchen. She was grateful Carlo had. There had been something provocative and arousing, with a touch of romance. Either way, it was precisely the elevated sexual punch and rush of excitement she wanted that Elliot never gave her.

Carlo pushed all the right buttons and made Soledad's uncharacteristic thrill-seeking—a breach of the disciplined, married woman—feel natural and rational. Then there were the mounds of reserves of energy she didn't know she had that Carlo uncovered, which helped keep up with a man eighteen years her junior.

Soledad couldn't remember the last time she'd felt so young and alive.

Now they sat on the deck of The Xanadu. Carlo looked gorgeous in khaki shorts, a crisp Polo shirt tucked into them, his warmly tanned face, a crown of windswept hair, and muscled arms. Sitting next to him, Soledad felt replete and complete, flattered that he chose her.

Under the sparkling sunbeams peeking out from dark clouds that had rolled in, they enjoyed the breakfast Mariela served of fried plantain, black beans, scrambled eggs, toast, fresh fruit, and a tall mimosa pitcher. Cheerful orange and purple birds of paradise speared from a brown vase at the centre of the teak table.

"You told me your husband had not brought you flowers in ages, and you deserve flowers, Soledad Thomas. A beautiful flower for a beautiful woman," Carlo said, tearing off most of the stem and tucking the flower in the hair that tumbled in waves around her face and over her shoulders, as he liked.

"They're lovely, thank you." Soledad reached up and traced fingers over it. "You're lovely." She tasted the sweetness of the mimosa on his lips when she kissed him.

"You look beautiful this morning." Carlo admired the contrast of the peach lace tank top against her tanned skin, but the confidence radiating from her eyes was what struck him most.

Sinking back in her chair, Soledad frowned thoughtfully. "I'm guessing you say that to all the women you take to bed, and judging from the closet stocked with provocative women's clothing, that count is pretty high."

"Yes, it is true that I tell all the women who fill my bed they are beautiful." Carlo flashed her a quick smile when her brow winged high. "But with you, they are not just words. I mean every word." He played his mouth over hers.

"Of course you do."

Both looked at the gleaming blue ocean for a short moment. The smell of the incoming rain was in the air, and a strong wind blowing from the east was making the waters turn restless.

"I enjoyed last night." Carlo halved a chocolate-covered strawberry. "Did you, Soledad Thomas?"

Soledad parted her lips for him to set the strawberry between them. "I did, and I enjoyed our early morning shower if you call it that. We could pick up where we left off after breakfast." Soledad crossed her legs, making the short, white pleated skirt ride high on her thighs. "We could."

The sexual innuendo in Soledad's eyes and the measured move to draw his attention made Carlo smile. Tender loving care and flattery, the great balm, had worn down the line between insecurity and confidence.

Appreciating the rebirth of Soledad Thomas, Carlo said, "Confidence looks great on you."

"It feels great, and it's due to you, so thank you."

The soulful sound of reggae music floated from the resort. The sound of slow and steady lapping of seawater mingled with gawking seagulls, parrots, and every tropical bird flitting from palm tree to palm tree.

"My pleasure." No longer concerned about the niceties, Soledad rose and sat on Carlo's lap. "You are not concerned anyone will see you, a married woman, doing the unthinkable with a man?"

Shaking her head, Soledad ran her fingers through his hair. "It adds excitement to the moment, don't you think?"

"I like the way your mind works." Carlo skimmed a fingertip along her jaw and slid it under her chin. "And I like hearing you say my name like a prayer as you did last night."

Suddenly Soledad saw the movie stream of their night together play out in her head, and she smiled. The things Carlo did to her body with his hands and mouth had her moaning his name, crying out in approval, and begging him never to stop with unrestrained abandon. That was a first for Soledad.

When the furry handcuffs came out this morning, her heart took one hard leap into her throat until Carlo cuffed himself to the shower bar and told her he was her prisoner to do with as she wished. The sexual thrill and sense of control made her feel empowered.

"You drive me crazy, Soledad Thomas." Carlo's lips cruised down the valley between her breasts. He got a whiff of the powdery soap he'd used to lather the honey off her body, a spear of pure lust shot to his groin, and he went rock hard.

An aroused male body drove her crazy, but she kept that tidbit to herself. A pinch of mystery always adds lustre to a woman.

Carlo was pleased Soledad didn't swat his hand away when he loosened the lace of her top to expose her breasts. Her ripe breasts spilled over the lacy edge, and he took them with his greedy mouth.

Soledad let out a shaky breath when the flash of heat washed over her. "God, you're good," she mumbled, gasping for air.

"You make me good." His teeth caught and nipped at her nipples and made her blood sing under her skin.

She threw her head back with a moan. The rain that came down in a straight easy fall from dark clouds showered over Soledad's face. "Show me another way I make you good?"

Carlo sent her a quick smile, and skimming his hands over her thigh, he awakened nerves and kindled needs in anticipation of what was coming.

The quick dip in her belly, the strong spear of lust, made her hot and wet. Her blood roared in her head when his fingers slid into the moist heat.

"You are not wearing panties." With a wicked smile on her face, she shook her head. "I like this confident Soledad very much."

She straddled him. "Me too," she said with quickened breaths when his expert fingers stroked.

"You like that?"

She tried to formulate a verbal response, but her brain failed to connect thought with speech as he slid his fingers and built the pressure to drive her to orgasm.

"Does that feel good?"

"God! Yes! Yes!" she whispered in between gasped breaths.

"Not yet, Soledad," he said when he felt her self-control slipping from her grasp. "I, too, am enjoying this as much as you are."

Her heart drumming in her ears, she caught her bottom lip between her teeth.

His fingers were rough on her, but his strokes, confident and firm, drove incredible, shocking rippled through her. Carlo knew where and how to touch her—a fine skill he possessed. Elliot had never filled her with such a euphoric sensation in their entire married life. If only Elliot were willing to listen and try to meet her needs when they made love, he'd fill her with the pleasure Carlo did.

Maybe the adventure of the illicit sexual relationship with a man younger than her made the experience exhilarating, although she doubted it. Carlo was passionate about her, and pleasing her more than satisfying himself was what elevated their lovemaking. If Elliot gave to her as much as Carlo did, Soledad wouldn't be here now. She was here because Elliot drove her to it.

"Are you ready to fly, amore?" He murmured, focused on her face.

Her heart thumped hard against her chest. "Yes, I can't hold off much longer."

"Say my name like a prayer as you did last night, *amore*." Soledad heard him say through the buzzing in her ears, and she did when her body shuddered to multiple orgasms.

Her body saturated with pleasure, she reached for the snap on his shorts. "I want to feel you inside me."

He flashed her a smile. "I hoped you'd say that." Carlo moved fast to free himself.

Wrapping his hands around her waist, he lifted her hips and lowered her. She gasped in delight when he pierced her and drove deep into her.

Lighting split dark clouds, and the thunder roared seconds before the wall of rain came down on them hard and unrelenting, but it didn't stop him. He thrust himself hard into her under the light of the next flash and hammered the orgasm through her. He flew with her and emptied into her, never leaving her smiling eyes.

Slaked, she buried her face in his neck, and for a long while, they remained, as they were, with the rain falling over them.

"How would you like to go for a sail?" Carlo smoothed back the wet hair clinging to her face. "I know a secluded beach where we can spend the morning doing whatever comes to mind."

Soledad's curious blue eyes looked at Carlo's face drenched with falling rain. "Sounds like fun, but it's raining, and that dark sky doesn't look good. And isn't September the prime hurricane season around these parts?"

"Certainty isn't everything, amore, and those are minor details."

"You're the adventurous type. Me, not so much."

"You could be." Carlo angled a look at Soledad. "I like hearing my name on your lips."

"Don't change the subject. I'm not sure we should sail…."

He played his mouth over hers to silence her. "How bad can it be, *amore*, if we were cast adrift in the middle of the ocean on The Xanadu?"

That Italian accent could make her jump into a fiery volcano if he asked her to. "Do you know how to handle this thing under those conditions?"

"I have been sailing for most of my life. I will take good care of you. Do you trust me, Soledad?"

She didn't have to think for long to answer him. "I do, with my life."

Carlo wiped the rain from her face and brushed his lips over hers. "Shall we sail and set off on the next adventure?"

Her stomach knotted at the idea of steering into a storm. Still, she couldn't deny it presented an irresistible element of danger and unpredictability to her humdrum life, and she nodded.

Chapter 21

TO CALM HIMSELF, Elliot paced the bedroom.

He was a problem solver, he told himself. As much as his father refused to accept it, it was what he did, and he needed to solve the problem under his roof. He had to find Soledad before word reached his father that she was missing.

It was why Elliot hadn't said anything to Jasmine about Soledad's disappearance. Jasmine was too close to her grandfather not to say anything. Working for him, she'd feel an obligation to tell him the minute Elliot relayed the news.

The disappointment in Charles's eyes and the condemnation to follow for Elliot's inability to control his wife would be swift. "How do you expect to manage my company when you can't manage the drama under your roof?" Charles would question in the imperial tone he reserved solely for Elliot.

Elliot managed a staff of hundreds at Thomas and Partners with precision and a firm hand. As the COO, Elliot increased revenue by twenty-five percent by forming the profitable forensics accounting division. Elliot had the respect of staff and clients, but not his father.

Nothing Elliot did ever pleased his overly demanding father.

Soledad often told Elliot to put Thomas and Partners behind him and start his own accounting firm. "You have the education, the knowledge, and the expertise. You can be your own man, Elliot."

Needing to prove his worth and earn his father's much-needed validation, Elliot hadn't taken heed of Soledad's advice and continued to endure the stress of his father's unreasonable demands. It was never enough for Charles Winston Thomas to increase revenue, decrease expenses, recruit the best minds, and bring in profitable clients. More, more, and more wasn't enough for him.

Recognition formed in Elliot's dark eyes, and he saw now how he'd brought that tension home with him every day and unloaded on his closest target and the only person who would listen, Soledad.

But Goddamn it, Soledad never complained, never made an issue of his thoughtlessness. She never said anything, whined, or made an issue of his long workdays. Elliot wished Soledad had. He wasn't a mind reader.

Huffing a breath in sheer frustration, Elliot paced the bedroom. He might be able to negotiate million-dollar deals, but as a man, he was deficient in the workings of the female mind. He'd demand a how-to-figure-out-women capsule implanted on his frontal lobe in his next life.

Elliot studied himself in the mirror. He barely recognized the man who stared back. Character lines fanned from his eyes. Gray threaded through his cropped hair, and the clean-shaven face had replaced the dark, long, unkempt hair and scruffy stubble of his youth.

Christ! He was old.

His face was etched with the lines and crevices brought on by the pressures of life. He carried twenty additional pounds on the once runners frame. Worse than all those changes was the hopelessness he saw in the eyes of a man once filled with dreams and adventure.

Elliot wasn't the once carefree, idealistic dreamer. He was no longer the man who protested the unjust and slept on a grass bed staring at the stars when the feeling suited. He was no longer the type of man who impulsively hopped into his car and drove cross-country for no reason other than adventure.

Elliot was a man with a wife, five children, a dog, and a home in the suburbs. He was a man with a mortgage who played hockey on Saturday night to let off steam and afterward went out for a drink with the boys. Elliot was a man who had responsibilities, loads of responsibility.

It's what happened to grownups, and Soledad knew it, he told himself.

Soledad wasn't any longer the wide-eyed, high-spirited girl with endless energy who'd fired him up with unbridled carnality. Grant it, she had five children she was responsible for, but that didn't compare to the pressures of running a multi-million dollar company.

Elliot provided Soledad with a beautiful home and a comfortable life. She had her bank accounts and time to do as she wished. What more could Soledad ask for?

Elliot kept his end of the bargain, and running away from home was how Soledad repaid him.

Maybe his father was right, Elliot told himself. How was he to manage the company when he couldn't control what went on in his home?

Elliot had to find Soledad and put everything under his roof right again.

Chapter 22

DRY AND CHANGED into a dusty pink off-the-shoulder tee and white shorts, Soledad made her way to the galley while Carlo, on deck, hoisted the sails and did whatever had to be done to set off on their adventure.

In the galley, Soledad stored the mounds of food and bottles of wine Carlo had Mariela bring from the resort in the cupboards and the refrigerator. If they were caught in a storm in the middle of the ocean, they wouldn't go hungry or thirsty, she thought.

Everything in its place, Soledad looked around for a moment. All the comforts of home with a touch of luxury, Soledad thought of the long dark-wood cabinets, stainless steel refrigerator, stovetop, a built-in oven and microwave. A padded bench and mahogany table faced the rectangular picture window above the double sink that looked out to the expanse of blue water and a darkening sky.

The boat rocked under her feet as the brackish waters became rougher under the propelling gust of wind. Her heart jumped—a little. The romance and fantasy of casting adrift in a storm with Carlo had Soledad feeling as if a spark fanned to life in her. She was on adventure-adrenalin overload. It was a feeling she wasn't used to, and Christ, it felt amazing.

Leaving the tidy kitchen, Soledad headed to the bedroom. She opened the briefcase Mariela had brought from her room and packed away her clothes. Next, Soledad made the bed where she and Carlo had tangled all night. His scent, all around her, shot a deep, penetrating warmth that wrapped around her heart and dazed her.

Soledad would never be able to make do with what she had before Carlo.

She was broken, and Carlo cemented her together. He filled her heart, mind, and soul with beautiful things. Carlo fulfilled her physical needs and gave her the ego boost she needed.

He made her feel like a wanted, desirable woman and stole her heart. Soledad was falling in love with him.

MILES FROM THE RESORT, CARLO DROPPED anchor in the turquoise waters of Paradise Island, and paradise it was. Low-lying mountains shaped the brown backdrop. A haze of green forest gleaming with dew at their base encircled them. A sandy beach lay white against the verge of cerulean waters.

On shore now, Carlo and Soledad set off to explore the secluded island. Taking the carved path into the woods, they hiked the picturesque south side of El Gato Mountain. Light dappled through the trees. The collective smells of life and decaying plants and wood, earth and soil hung thick in the clammy air.

Carlo stopped and turned to Soledad. "Listen."

She listened to the silence until it was interrupted with the chatter of birds and flutter of wings as they shot out from the treetops when Carlo clapped his hands.

"The forest goes silent when the wildlife detects foreign life." Carlo clapped his hands again. "Listen now."

Soledad heard the twitter of birds, the gibber of monkeys, and the scream of peacocks. Crows cawed, frogs croaked, and parrots squawked. Soledad was happy not to hear the growls of tigers or howls of wolves.

"It's amazing," she said, thinking that until now, the most exotic thing she'd experienced was the grilled octopus at the Pier 1 restaurant.

They walked the narrow dirt path for three miles when Carlo stopped. "This here is what I wanted to show you. What do you think?"

Eyes popping wide, Soledad looked around her and took it all in. "It's stunning."

Amid the jungle of green, spreading like a thick carpet and the trees spearing toward the sky, the waterfall's roar spilling from a dizzying height into the lagoon was nothing short of spectacular.

A flock of pink flamingos waded along the lagoon's banks, and further in, ducks glided along its mirror-smooth surface. A luscious spread of tropical flowers, abundant and bright with colour, danced in concert with the palm trees that ringed the lagoon's impossibly clear, blue water. In a spectral of vibrant colours, freshwater fish skimmed its sandy bottom or swam in schools.

Carlo pointed and named every species of fish. "The orange fish with glittery blue stripes are known as paradise fish. I made sure to stock all the freshwater lakes on the island with them."

"You stocked them?"

Carlo snapped a bright yellow hibiscus with a red centre and tucked it in her hair. "Them and all the other fish you find on the island lagoons, rivers, and lakes. This is my island, inherited from my grandmother, of course. I think it came from husband number four or maybe five. It is hard to keep track of Nonna Sofia's love life. Anyway, he was a conservationist who wanted to safeguard many places such as this for the local wildlife."

Taking it all in, she smiled at him. "My twins would love you. They too aim to safeguard the planet, places like these, from destruction."

"It sounds as if they have plans, good plans." He signalled her to sit on the rock, and she was glad to get off her feet. Although her backpack was half the size of Carlo's, it was beginning to weigh heavy. At times like these, she hated her ageing body.

"All my children have plans." The heat felt heavy, and Soledad took a sizeable sip of water from the offered water bottle.

"And lead their own lives." Carlo took a pull of water when she turned the bottle over.

Soledad nodded. "When they're young, your tired mind wishes they were older and led independent lives. When they reach the age of independence, you wish they needed you."

"That is how it is with children." Carlo reached into his backpack and pulled out two sandwiches.

"You're wise for a childless man."

"Not really. It is common sense. Lobster roll or lobster roll. Good choice," he said when she reached for the wrapped roll in his left hand. "Right now, though, is the time to focus on you and do what you have always wanted."

"I don't know how to. I've been focused on my children, Elliot, and my home for most of my adult life."

Carlo snapped two collapsible glasses open and poured wine from the thermos he retrieved from his backpack. "This is your time, Soledad Thomas, and focusing on yourself is what you need to do."

"I have no friends to share my interests with, and Elliot has no interest in sharing time with me." There was no hiding from Carlo her feeling of abject loneliness and the emptiness she felt. "You know, when I was young, there was so much I wanted to do with my friends, but there was no money. Now that I have the financial means, there are no friends to do anything with."

Carlo looked into her guileless eyes as she absently bit into her lobster roll and said, "I'm sorry, Soledad, I...."

Soledad held up a hand to cut Carlo off. "You have nothing to apologize for. You're lovely, and this is lovely. I love being with you, Carlo. I..."

"That's El Gato." Carlo pointed to the waterfall cascading from the peak of the mountain. "Meaning the cat because if you angle your head right, it looks like...."

"A cat's head, I see it."

"This water is always a balmy seventy-five degrees." Carlo shed his clothes and feet from the cascading waterfall, dove into the blue water of the lagoon. "Join me, Soledad."

Soledad grinned a wide grin. Rising, she took all of her clothes off and dived in. When she surfaced, Soledad lifted her arms to hook around his neck. "I've never skinny-dipped before."

"Same with me." Carlo's mouth lifted at one corner, and she threw back her head and laughed.

The fish swam around them, forming a sort of ceremonial circle. "Should I be worried about them?"

"They may decide to venture into parts unknown, so best you tighten your buttocks." Carlo flashed her a wicked grin, and Soledad responded with a snorted laugh. Her wet hair scooped back, fell straight down her shoulders. All Carlo could do was stare. "You are very beautiful, Soledad Thomas, and sexy." There was nothing more he could say to make her ego swell any bigger, Soledad thought. "And a great lover." And yet he did.

Soledad framed Carlo's face with her hands. "You do things to me, wonderful, beautiful things, and I'm not just talking about the fantastic sex."

"I am good at the sex." Carlo nibbled on her earlobe, fed at her neck, and followed it with skimming butterfly kisses over her wet shoulders.

"Yes, you are very good at that."

If Elliot had half of Carlo's skill, she wouldn't be here with another man. If Elliot didn't see his penis as a mere body ornament, she wouldn't be sleeping with a man she'd just met—and falling in love with him.

Soledad rested her forehead against his. "But it's much more than the great sex. You have me doubting everything I know, everything real in my life."

Being there with Carlo was too comfortable, and Soledad's mind drifted from comfort to doubt because when things were too good to be true, they weren't.

Was it love or infatuation she felt? Maybe the heightened sense of romance she hadn't felt in so long, tinged with the hunger in a man's eyes for her, and a man's touch on her body, sparked the emotion of love.

When he saw the expression on her face that spoke of love, he said, "As I have told you, Soledad, you must not fall in love with me for obvious reasons."

"I can't help feeling this way." They were lovers, and she could handle the guilt of their physical connection, but the emotional whirlwind Carlo set off in her was an unexpected sensation muddying her mind.

"I know this, my love, but you must not. You have a family and a husband waiting for you."

Soledad felt immensely sad at the thought, and her eyes cut away from his.

Carlo slid his fingers under her chin and turned her face until their eyes met. "For now, you are here with me, and I will help you placate your need for adventure. I will give you the excitement you need, but you must promise you will not fall in love with me."

"How do you always know what I'm thinking when you don't know me? Not really."

Carlo didn't need to know Soledad for long to know who she was. He didn't need to ask her the questions to know what her thoughts were or where she came from. Carlo didn't ask, not because he wasn't interested, but because those weren't the questions she wanted to be asked. Soledad knew who she was. She knew her responsibilities and where she came from. Soledad knew what she wanted.

Right then, what she needed was to infuse adventure with a pinch of danger into her humdrum life—if only for a few days. Soledad needed a sexual fling with a man who made her feel desirable and wanted.

Soledad was typical of the women who vacationed alone at his resort. They were women desperate for attention and validation. They were women who left behind a life that made them feel as if they were underwater, struggling for air with no surface in sight.

For the few days on Topaz Island, the women who came wanted to shed their persona and fill their lonely lives with the excitement and adventure they lacked.

If that was what Soledad wanted, that was what Carlo would give her, no judgement, no questions asked, or strings attached.

Carlo's gaze flicked to Soledad and looked deep into her eyes. "I do know you, Soledad Thomas. The trials of love, loyalty, and devotion are easy to see on your face, *amore*." His mouth met hers to silence her. "No more words. We are here for your pleasure. How would you like to tick the, Make Love In A Lagoon box off your bucket list?"

"I like the way you think, Mr. Moretti."

He pulled her in and covered her mouth with his. His tongue dancing with hers, Soledad tasted excitement and danger, everything she wanted.

It didn't take long for the glint in her eyes to turn into a grin when Carlo made the orgasm burst like thunder in her system. Her boisterous cries sent the birds scattering from the treetops.

Amid the beauty surrounding them, Soledad nuzzled his neck and wondered how she could give such a perfect man up.

Chapter 23

A THICK MANILA folder in one hand and her Burberry bag in the other, Jasmine walked into the kitchen and was ignored by her siblings. Up to no good, Jasmine thought as Noah tapped fingers on the laptop keyboard and the twins looked over his shoulders.

"Hey, squirt, twinsies, sup?" Jasmine raised her voice over the clanking of the keyboard to get their attention. Definitely up to good, she determined when the three simultaneously looked up with guilt-ridden eyes. "What are you guys doing that you shouldn't be?"

Annie stepped up to say, "You're too old to be saying 'sup,' and the question is, what are you doing here, Miss Professional?" Annie's eyes narrowed as she studied Jasmine.

Her hair tied into a smooth updo brought out the steel-blue eyes shadowed in bronze makeup, the rosy dusted high cheekbones and glossed full lips. Freckles sprinkled over her nose and cheeks on a perfect complexion resulting from a strict hydrating regime and monthly facials. In the magenta dress, crop jacket, and black pumps, Jasmine looked every bit the professional woman.

"I don't think she's too old to be saying 'sup.' Sup, Jasmine?"

"Thank you, Allie, and for your information, evil twin," Jasmine looked at Annie, "I'm here to drop this file for Daddy." Jasmine dropped the file and her bag on the table.

"He asked you to bring them?" Annie and Allie asked in chorus.

Jasmine reached into the cupboard for a glass. "No, Grandfather asked me to drop them off when Daddy didn't show up for the weekly morning briefing. Man, was Grandfather pissed when he didn't see Daddy at the boardroom table this morning. I got an earful when I couldn't tell Grandfather where Daddy was." She walked over to the refrigerator and pressed the glass to the water dispenser. "Where is Daddy, anyway? And where's Mom? What's for dinner? I'm starving."

"There's leftover pizza over there." Noah pointed to the counter. "Vegetarian, of course, only these two dipshits like that crap."

Annie slapped Noah on the head. "Language dip wad."

"Don't do that. My head is a delicate and necessary instrument of my person."

"Says the hockey player who risks getting his head bashed during every game." Allie slapped her brother on the head now.

"I swear to God, you hit me once more and…."

"Children, stop. You guys have store-bought pizza on taco night. Mom would never allow that. Now I know something is going on. Daddy misses a day of work, a briefing with Grandfather, which he'd only do when hell froze over, and Mom's not here. Spill. Now." Jasmine aimed probing eyes at her siblings.

"I gotta go." Annie made a quick exit out of the kitchen, and Allie followed close behind.

"Hey, get back here, you two," Jasmine called out, but the twins were quick on their feet and disappeared up the stairs. "Oh, no, you don't squirt." Jasmine clamped a hand on Noah's shoulders when he came straight out of the chair and held him down

"You're hurting me. You never did have respect for the tenets of martial arts. You know you're not supposed to use your Karate skills to cause unjustifiable harm."

Jasmine cocked an eyebrow. "This is justified. Tell me what's going on, Noah."

"I don't know nothing."

"Anything, and you always know everything going on around in this house. So, spill." Jasmine clamped down harder on his shoulder when he didn't speak.

"Jesus, Jasmine, I'm your baby brother, your only brother who will carry the Thomas name."

"Not a selling point, and if you recall, I could always beat your ass when we were younger. Imagine what I could do to you now with a black belt under me."

"I should have listened to Mom and taken karate instead of hockey when she suggested it."

"Should've, would've." Jasmine glanced at the search display on Noah's computer screen of hospitals and morgues.

"You're getting a bit morbid there, squirt."

Noah let out a long breath. "Me and the twins...."

"The twins and I," Jasmine corrected.

Noah rolled his eyes to the sky. "Do you want to know what's going on or not?"

"Go on."

"The twins and I were calling the hospitals and morgues looking for mom."

Jasmine's hand went weak, and she released her hold on Noah's shoulder. "Why? Why are you calling the hospitals and morgues looking for mom?" The words were tinged with genuine panic.

"You need to talk to Dad." Noah massaged the pinched nerve out of his shoulder.

Instant distress ran across her face. "Why? What's happened?"

"You need to talk to Dad," Noah repeated, flexing his shoulder.

"Where is he?"

"In his office. Go…." Jasmine was out of the kitchen before Noah finished saying, "easy on him. Man, am I happy she's out of this house, and I have only two crazy sisters left to deal with."

Chapter 24

CARLO AND SOLEDAD made it back to The Xanadu minutes before the sky went completely dark, and the clouds burst open and let the rain come down hard.

Nestled in Carlo's arms, they lay in bed quietly for a time listening to the sound of thunder rumbling, rain battering the deck above, and the ocean waves thrashing The Xanadu.

"Are you scared, Soledad?" Contemplative, Carlo eyed her. She had a lovely rosy glow on her face from the aftermath of her shower. Her mink-coloured hair tumbled carelessly around her face making her look like a siren emerged from the angry sea.

Soledad shook her head. Nestled in the warmth of his arms, she felt protected and safe. "Not as long as I'm with you." She watched the lightning that chased the boom of thunder cut the darkened sky and the rise and role of waves in the tumultuous ocean lashed by a gale-force wind.

"You are a woman who enjoys danger."

"Not until I met you. Until you, the most dangerous experience in my life was putting too much hot pepper in my tomato sauce. I must admit getting a taste of it is thrilling."

Carlo gave Soledad one long, quiet study. "By that, you mean the thrill of us?"

Soledad tipped her face up to Carlo. "I do."

As sobering as it was, Soledad put all thoughts of the children and Elliot to the back of her mind, and her focus was Carlo. She felt no remorse or regret because living in the moment's excitement with Carlo was what mattered now. Carlo made her happy and filled the widening hole in her heart.

"You make me feel alive, desirable, and wanted. I haven't felt that way in a long, long time. For too long, I've lived with the unspoken obsolescence. I'm a wife with an absent husband, a mother with grown children who forget I exist. My only friend is a five-year-old pug, and he shamelessly abandons me like a chewed boned when the washing machine comes on. That's a story for another day." Soledad rolled over to face him. "Now, I have a bounce in my step because of you. I've regained my confidence, and I like who I am."

Soledad recognized that as much as Carlo rescued her from her descent into despair and helped her regain her confidence, he'd unlocked a new set of complications. Soledad gave that some thought and decided the pros of making Carlo a permanent part of her life outweighed the negatives.

Carlo saw everything she imagined she wanted in that one moment and said, "You must not put me above your family, *amore*. That is not what this is."

"What is this, Carlo? What is this between us?"

"As much as I desire you, this is about fulfilling your fantasy, needs, and wants." Propping himself on his arm, Carlo eased the bedsheet from her shoulders and lowered it below her breasts. "I like to look at you." His eyes roved over her in a way that made her cheeks tinge pink, and she reached for the bedsheet to cover herself. Carlo stopped her. "Do not be embarrassed, *amore*. You are a beautiful woman."

Soledad smiled, pleased with the accolade she never tired of hearing.

"Have you ever made love on a rocking boat?" Carlo circled his fingertips over the curve of her breast, caressing her nipple until it hardened.

"Never."

"Would you like to?"

"Very much. I sense you'll make it feel like romance on water."

"If that is what you would like, it is how I will make it feel for you. And spoiler alert, the bouncing waves will make the lovemaking more seamless." He gave her a beaming grin. "But it will feel very romantic and exciting, which you told me is what you want in your life, yes?" Soledad nodded. "With a touch of danger, of course, as you like," he added when the boat rocked enough to feel like they were about to roll off the bed.

Carlo feathered his fingertip along her jaw and slid it under her chin. "I want to fill your life with everything you want, and I want to fulfill your fantasies and share in the moment with you."

Knowing that added a deeper emotional element to the experience. Soledad looked at him and touched his face. She fell deeper in love with this beautiful man lying next to her with every passing hour. She wanted to tell him. Soledad wanted to use her newly found large, rich voice to say to the world how deeply in love she was with him, but Carlo was serious about the covertness of their relationship, and it wouldn't come to pass—not yet.

"Can we just lie here for a bit?"

"Of course, *amore*."

Soledad rested her head on the hard plane of Carlo's chest. Basking in the warmth and comfort of him, Soledad closed her eyes to work out her confused thoughts.

Chapter 25

ELLIOT'S HEAD JERKED up from his folded arms when Jasmine stormed into his office like a tornado. "Jesus, Jasmine, you startled me."

Jasmine studied Elliot. He looked as if he hadn't slept in days. He had a good growth of stubble going, his hair could use a comb, and his clothes were rumpled. "You look … tired, Daddy."

Elliot ran a hand, hands over his face. "What are you doing here?"

"Grandfather asked me to drop off the Wingate file. He wants you to go over it tonight, so you're ready for tomorrow's meeting."

"Shit, that's tomorrow." He screwed up his face as his fingers raked at his hair. "Well, I'm not going to make it in for that meeting,"

Jasmine's shock was clear on her face. Now she knew there was something seriously amiss. Her father forgot a meeting with a client as important as Jacob Wingate was a first. Panic set in.

"What's going on, Daddy? You don't show up to work. You forgot your weekly briefing with Grandfather. Grandfather!" She stretched the word for emphasis. "Noah and the twins are contacting the hospitals and morgues and won't tell me why."

"I didn't know they were doing that." Elliot reached for the bottle on his desk and found it empty.

"Yet, they are, and I can't see Noah setting aside his gaming and the twinsies not stream about every minutia of their lives to fill their day with cold calling the hospitals and morgues. Mom's not home and you look like a mess. What's going on?"

Elliot couldn't talk his way out of this. Jasmine was much like him, and she'd push until she got answers. He'd have to tell Jasmine everything and risk the news of Soledad's disappearance reaching his father. He stood to lose everything he'd worked for, his job, the company, his inheritance. His father would ensure his weak son never got his hands on what Elliot rightfully deserved.

"Your mother's gone," Elliot said after a short silence.

"Gone, what do you mean gone?"

"She wasn't here when we got home. "This will explain everything." He reached into his desk drawer and handed Jasmine Soledad's note, which he came close to tossing in the fire in the hearth after his drinking binge earlier in the day.

Jasmine read Soledad's handwritten note and fell silent for a moment. "I can't believe I forgot. I was too wrapped up with work, with the hiring of Grandfather's fourth assistant in five years." Not her job, but no one said no to Charles Winston Thomas. "Then there's the software upgrade and security protocols I've been working to put in place to avoid another breach of our database, and…."

Jasmine produced a long list of excuses to appease her guilty mind and, in the process, recognized what she hadn't until then. Her grandfather was drawing her into his web of the unreasonable twenty-four-seven workload he demanded of her father. It dialled up her worry level to red. As much as Jasmine loved her work, she didn't want to enslave herself to her grandfather as her father had. Jasmine saw how her grandfather's perverse expectations consumed Elliot over the years and now drove her mother from their home.

"You had to see this coming, Daddy?"

Remorse bubbled into anger, and Elliot barked, "Of course, I didn't, and your mother never said anything. She never complained." Elliot stormed out of the office in search of a drink.

Jasmine followed her father to the living room. "She never does, Daddy. To her detriment, Mom never complains about anything."

"I'm not a Goddamn mind reader, Jasmine." Elliot reached for the bottle of brandy on the console table behind the long, chocolate sofa and poured it liberally into a glass.

"She must have been heartbroken. I can't remember Mom forgetting our birthdays." Jasmine turned to Elliot. "You, Daddy, yes, Mom never. She deserves better from us, from you."

Elliot flicked guilt-laden eyes away from his daughter toward the marble fireplace. She watched him silently add logs and spur a fire to glow. Soledad always liked the warmth and smell that a fire in the hearth brought to the living room.

Jasmine fell back on the sofa. "I don't remember Mom not baking a cake or planning a celebration for our birthdays or any minor event in our lives. I don't remember Mom not being there for us when we needed her. And this was her fiftieth birthday. She must have felt so let down by all of us."

"Christ, what's the big deal about this birthday?" Elliot's voice was raw with fatigue.

She looked at him for a time without speaking. Men were so dense. How they were in positions of power instead of women was the million-dollar question Jasmine wanted answered?

"It's not the birthday per se, Daddy. It's where it's leading, the major looming changes." Jasmine proceeded to explain when a blank look registered on his face. "The oncoming change of life, us leaving home and making her feel lonesome, and you're not there for her. You can't possibly be when you're putting twelve to fourteen-hour days at the office. When was the last time you took her to dinner or brought her flowers?" Jasmine watched his mouth twist. "She must feel rejected, sad, and alone. Our, your, dismissal of her drove her to leave."

Elliot's shoulders hunched, his face filled with a kind of knowing. Jasmine suspected he'd known the truth but refused to accept it.

"But forget about all that right now, Daddy. What's the police have to say?"

He looked away and down to the drink in his hand.

Of course, he hadn't called the police. He'd been too busy drinking his guilt away. "Christ, Daddy, you should have called them the minute you found her missing." Jasmine rounded on him.

His lips trembled for fifteen seconds before he firmed them and lashed out at his daughter. "Don't use that tone with me, young lady. I'm still your father."

"Sorry, Daddy, but why haven't you called the police?"

"For one, your mother left of her own accord." Elliot took a sizeable, numbing gulp of his drink. "Two, she has to go missing for twenty-four hours before they consider her a missing person."

She interrupted. "One, that twenty-four-hour thing is a load of crap they push on television shows. Two, it's been two days since she left, which takes it to forty-eight hours." Jasmine kept her voice even, but her eyes narrowed with impatience. "You haven't called them because of Grandfather."

Elliot leaned forward in his seat. Resting his elbows on his thighs, he held his glass in both hands and stared into it quietly.

"Yeah, that's what I thought because that's what it's always about, Daddy, keeping Grandfather out of the loop of your failure. You didn't want this getting back to him for fear of his judgement. It's the only reason you haven't called them. Isn't that true?" Jasmine paused and waited for a response, but Elliot remained silent. "Fine, I'll call them."

Elliot knocked the drink back. "I'll call them. She's my wife." Goddamn Soledad, there was no keeping this from his father now, he thought, reaching for his phone.

Chapter 26

IT FELT FOOLISHLY romantic to lay twined together in bed in the darkened room and ride out the storm. Wrapped in the safety of Carlo's arms, with rocking waves thrashing the boat, Soledad listened to the crack and boom of thunder and the rain and wind lashing at the window. They watched the flash of lightning slicing and lighting the sky and bedroom like a strobe light and talked.

The conversation ranged over many subjects but skirted that of her family, husband, home life, and her state of mind. Carlo didn't press. It wasn't out of a sense of caution he didn't, but because he understood, she wasn't ready to disclose much about herself. Right then, Soledad needed comforting and a listening ear, and that's what he gave her.

Soledad sipped piña colada from the thermos Carlo prepared in anticipation of storm watching. "You've certainly thought of everything."

He kissed her on the nose. "It is not my first circus."

A smile played across her face. "I think you mean rodeo."

"I know this. I just like to see you smile." Carlo pulled her close and brushed his mouth to hers. "Are you happy to be here with me, Soledad?"

"Very much so." Deliberately, she cast blue eyes to the vast sea, lashing rolls of frothing water about.

"Have I made your fiftieth birthday a more pleasant experience?" Carlo said, breaking the silence.

"How do you know it's my birthday or was?"

"I made it a point to know everything about you." He lifted a hand to push at her hair. Her skin had darkened under the sun adding more depth and colour to her brilliantly blue eyes.

Intrigued, she said, "Such as."

"I know you like sex and piña colada a lot." His eyes filled with amusement when her eyebrows quirked. "I know you've been feeling down, and connecting the dots led me to your fiftieth birthday as the reason." Carlo spooned his body to hers. "I am here to tell you that you have nothing to be upset about. You are in your prime and you, Soledad, are a beautiful woman, vibrant, and a very desirable woman."

"I know you're saying that to make me feel better."

"Why would you think that? I mean, you caught the eye of a thirty-two-year-old man."

"Well, there's no accounting for taste," she said, with an elbow jab to the ribs.

"And you've satisfied this thirty-two-year-old man's sexual appetite."

"Have I really satisfied you? I mean I'm not that experienced. I've only had one man in my life."

"You have satisfied me, in every way and wonderfully if I may say so." Carlo's fingers skimmed up and down her arm. Her skin tingled beneath his touch. "You have promised me you would stop doubting yourself." Carlo slid his fingers under Soledad's chin and turned her face to his. "You must keep your promise to me. Promise me, Soledad, you will stop second-guessing yourself."

"I promise."

"You are beautiful and very desirable." He'd said it many times to her before, but reaffirmation was crucial in her state of mind. "Add to that the fact you're caring and smart, as I imagine your children are," he said, nudging the door open to signal she could cross into the conversation she wanted to have but wouldn't.

She was quiet, and there was nothing awkward in the silence. Carlo knew Soledad was thinking of her children and Elliot, who, until then, she'd put to the back of her mind and needed to gather the strength to say what came next.

"They really are smart kids," Soledad said after a floating silence. "Hope, my oldest, is interning to become a cardiac surgeon. The same goes for her boyfriend, soon to become Mr. Hope Thomas, if she has it her way," Soledad said, after some time, her face lighting up with pride.

"A strong woman who knows what she wants."

"She does, as does Jasmine. She's second in line. She's already working as the assistant manager at a multi-million dollar company, but that's not enough for her. She aims to take over the full management of the firm. Grant it, it's her grandfather's company, my father-in-law, but she asks for no special treatment. She wants to earn her place on her own."

"A decisive woman. The pear does not seem to fall far from the tree."

Soledad's lips stretched out in a smile at the quirky comment. "The twins, Allie and Annie, are next in line. They're seventeen and still finding their way, but both are already doing everything they can to rescue the world from the grips of global warming."

"A most honourable goal. You have all girls?"

Soledad shook her head. "Noah is the youngest and my only boy."

"He is not as ambitious as the girls?"

"He's crossing over into manhood and dealing with...."

"Hormones," Carlo finished for her remembering his teen years and Sofia, Evelina, Maria and.... "Yes, hormones can make your head fuzzy for a long while. Hormonal tugs are still making my head dizzy." The words tapered off to a toothy smile. "You have been a busy woman doing the most important work, being a mama. You should be proud and pleased with your accomplishment. Your children sound like wonderful people."

Soledad looked over her shoulder at Carlo. "I have done a great job with them. My children are well adjusted, polite, productive, and kind. I'm proud of my children."

Now he heard the pride in her voice become louder. "Of course, you should be proud. Intelligent, ambitious children, you had a part in their making, and that is a special way to measure your life."

Soledad couldn't have said it better. Beaming a smile, she sat up next to him. "It is, isn't it?"

Even through her grin, Carlo could see she had more to say but hesitated. Deciding she was ready but needed a push to cross the line, he said, "You haven't mentioned your husband." Carlo shrugged out of the cocooning blanket and pushed himself to a sitting position against the bed's headboard. Bare-chested and in need of a shave, he looked good enough to eat. Soledad had to turn away to settle her thoughts and stared past him out the dark window.

The storm was abating, and the gilded light of the rising moon sheened light over the water. In the distance, Soledad thought she saw a pod of dolphins, surfacing and skimming over the water before diving.

"You can talk to me about him." Carlo unclasped the night table drawer, opened it, and reached for two protein bars. "Dinner," he said, holding them up for her to choose between the chocolate nut and crunchy peanut butter.

Soledad opted for the peanut butter and, unwrapping it, picked at it. "His name is Elliot. He's much older than you are and a tight-ass accountant. It's always been a wonder that he let me manage the house finances and income."

Carlo took a healthy bite of his chocolate nut bar. "He does not sound so bad. I have heard of worse husbands."

Of course, he'd say that. Protecting and standing together was the male mantra, Soledad thought. "I suppose. Accounting is his trade, but what he is, is the COO, the Chief Operating Officer, for his father's firm." She took the water bottle he turned over to her and sipped to wet her dry throat. "He ... forgot my birthday." She felt childish saying the words and waited for his reaction before saying anything further.

Carlo pushed back the hair that tumbled in waves over her shoulders and breasts. "That hurt you."

The man was too perfect to be true. Was it any wonder she was falling in love with him? "More disappointed than hurt. I mean, I understand he has responsibilities and a lot of pressure at work. Running the firm is a demanding job, and I know he works hard to provide for us." Soledad tried to convince herself, but Carlo could see the hurt in her eyes.

"Honesty, Soledad. Be honest not for me, but for yourself."

She rose from the bed and gave herself a moment to ensure the boat was settled. Minutes ago, it rolled and rocked, making it feel like it would capsize.

On level ground, Soledad reached for the black satin robe, wrapped her body with it, and walked to the window. Moonlight shimmered in hazy beams on the calming water like a flowing ribbon. Clouds were moving out, and a clear night sky was beginning to paint the view.

Carlo listened to the soundless distance between them until Soledad whirled to him. "I am angry and hurt and feel empty and alone. We've been married for too long for him to forget. We've lost our intimacy, our romance, our closeness. We barely touch or talk anymore. The least he could do is…."

"Acknowledge you," Carlo finished. That act of caring, of need, was a touchstone for Soledad, the last thread that held Elliot and her together. It was such a small act, and Elliot trivialized it or put it out of his mind as unnecessary.

"It's silly, I know, but I feel a hole in my existence."

Carlo stumbled into his jeans and walked to her. "It is not silly, not if it makes you feel bad about yourself."

Carlo wrapped his arms around her to acknowledge her and fill her emptiness. Soledad easily opened herself to what he gave her, what she needed to smooth over the feeling of rejection and loneliness. "I'm sorry to be burdening you with my emotional turmoil."

Radiating moonlight spread silver over her, and he lifted a hand and ran it over her hair. "You may talk. And I may listen. And miracles might happen."

"Hemingway," she said, and he nodded.

He said what she needed to hear and gave just what she needed, and her heart bloomed with love. She started to tell him that, but he covered her mouth with his to silence words she would regret later.

"Why won't you let me say the words I want to say to you?"

"I have told you, you must not fall in love with me. You have a life you must go back to."

She dropped her head to his shoulder. "I may not want to go back to that life."

"Whether you want to or not, you must. Everyone needs a place of love and safety, Soledad. Everyone wants recognition and to be appreciated. It is what you desire and what you are looking for, but you must be with your family to help you decide what you want from life. You need to be surrounded by your children and be with Elliot to help you determine which life, your existing one, or this one, will fill the next phase of your life. It is a big decision to make, *amore*, that you must not make lightly. But know this, Soledad Thomas, no one will love you as I do." He brought her hand to his beating heart.

Part III

The End

We create our destiny by our thoughts, wants, and needs.

— M.L. Lexi

Chapter 27

Fifty Hours Later

HOPE STEPPED BACK when the door she was about to stab her key into the lock opened and let the police by. Both police officers gave her a subtle tip of the head as they walked past her.

"I'm sorry I'm late, Daddy, but I had an emergency roll in as I was leaving," she said, looking into the face so much like hers.

Hope's shoulder-length hair, shades lighter than her father's, was knotted in a long braid. Loose wisps flowed around her pretty face down to her rosy cheeks. She wore blue scrubs under a waist-high black leather jacket, and the fuzzy pink socks were visible from the pockets of her Crocs.

"What did they say?" Hope closed the door behind her. "What are they planning to do? What's their next step?"

"Take a breath, honey." Elliot leaned in to kiss her on the cheek. The antiseptic smell of the hospital that lingered on her clothes came at him strongly. "You look tired," he said, looking into the shadowed dark eyes.

"A busy forty-eight-hour shift will do that. You look worn out." Hope shed her jacket and tossed it and her cross-body bag on the entryway table. "How are you holding up, Daddy? Are you alright?"

"No, I'm not alright, Hope. I'm just not."

Something so sad resonated in his eyes, and Hope leaned in to take him into a tight hug. "It's going to be alright, Daddy. We're going to find Mom. How about we get you some coffee?" she said when the smell of alcohol radiating from his body hit her.

"I don't need coffee. I'm fine."

The irritation that edged into Elliot's voice, the worried look on his face, the wrinkled shirt and jeans, and the tousled hair told Hope her father was far from okay. Hope followed him to the kitchen, where her siblings sat around the stressed oak table. At the center of the table, a carafe of coffee sat on a bamboo trivet. Next to it were a cow-shaped creamer, a sugar bowl, and two unused white cups.

Noah sat at the head of the table and sipped on the sugary pop he lived on. Next to him, the twins idly ran their spoons through the cereal in their bowl. Jasmine held the brandy snifter in both hands while worried eyes stared down at the amber liquid.

"Glad you could finally make it," Jasmine said, looking at Hope. The sarcasm rang clear in her voice.

"I had a GSW come in as I was leaving." Hope kissed Buddy's head when he excitedly lunged at her, his tail whirling like helicopter blades. "Would you prefer I left the victim bleeding to death? Then I had to wait for my replacement to relieve me, who ultimately was pulled into the OR. So I begged Ethan to step in. Heads up, he won't be here until much later." Hope slid her petite, slim frame into the vacant chair next to Allie.

"Woah, that's a gunshot wound." Noah's eyes went wide with admiration for his big sister.

Annie's eyebrow shot up. "You're a morbid little fuck, Noah."

"Are they going to remove the bullet or leave it in?" Noah asked.

"Jesus, Noah, shut the fuck up," Annie snapped.

That caused fainthearted Buddy to think better than to stick around, and he bounced from the room at lightning speed.

"Guys, stop it." Allie drew an exasperated breath in and let it out. "Now's not the time for this. Mom's gone missing. We all forgot her birthday, Daddy, and us, and hurt her, and she's not coming back." The tears sprang to her eyes, and Hope wrapped an arm around her sister and shushed.

"She'll be back, honey." Hope ran a soothing hand up and down Allie's back.

"You don't know that," Allie barked more out of fear than anger.

"Look at me." Hope pinched Allie's chin and tilted her face to meet hers. Dark eyes on innocent, blue eyes, she said, "She'll be back," in the soft, tender bedside voice she used to ease patients' anxieties. "She's as much as telling us that by leaving her clothes, purse, and credit cards behind. She's only ... stepped out for a breather. Grant it, a long one, but a breather nonetheless."

Jasmine's mouth twisted into a nonverbal Christ. "You've been inhaling Nitrous Oxide at that hospital of yours for too long."

"I know tempers and fear are flaring, but your sister's right. Your mother will be back. She took no money or anything that indicates she'd be away for long, and her passport is still in the safe." Elliot fished the lidded container with the leftover vegetarian pizza from the refrigerator.

"Daddy, you said it was her expired passport you found," Annie pointed out.

"It is, but she's efficient about shredding the old passports when she renews them." Elliot handed Hope the container.

"Pfft, really, Dad, shredding is what you're going with?" Noah rolled his eyes to the sky. "Even I could do better."

Elliot let his glance slide over at Noah for a moment. As much as the boy was his favourite, he couldn't rely on him for support. "Thank you for that, son." Elliot turned to Hope. "I figured you'd be hungry. It's vegetarian pizza."

Hope took the container from Elliot. "Thanks, Daddy. I am. I haven't eaten since this morning." She removed the lid from the Tupperware and popped it into the microwave for one minute. "

"Why don't you guys go to your rooms?" Elliot looked over at Noah and the twins.

"We're not going anywhere, Dad," Allie said with unusual sharpness. "Although it's mostly your fault Mom's gone, Daddy, we all had a hand in her disappearance."

Elliot closed his eyes and endeavoured to squash the guilt. "Thank you for that, Allie."

"Well, it is your fault, Dad," Allie said, her voice uncharacteristically rising, hardening. "We're the kids. You're the grown-up. You should know better. Isn't that what you're always telling us? How's that working out for you, Dad?" Allie's lit eyes latched onto her father and gave him a moment to respond. Nothing. "Whatever you have to say, I want to hear. I'm sorry, Daddy, but I don't trust you to take care of this. Besides, I'm a part of this family and part of the problem."

Much respect for her meek sister, Annie thought. "That includes you." Annie clamped a hand on Noah's shoulder as he started to rise.

"But, Dad said we could go and that Mom will be back soon. There's a Call Of Duty epic game starting in ten minutes." Noah brooded.

"Sit down, Noah." The twins ordered in unison.

"I hate the two of you with the strength of a thousand suns." Sulking, Noah fell back into his chair.

"The twins are right, Dad," said Jasmine. "Let's fill Hope in on what the police said, and let's put our heads together and figure out what we need to do to find Mom."

Chapter 28

SOLEDAD TURNED FROM the window and walked to the dresser. "I'm not ready to go home. Not yet." She needed time to decide. "I don't know if I'll ever be ready. Besides, I have two days left of my vacation, and I intend to enjoy them." She opened the drawer, reached for the brush and ran it through her hair.

"You do, and I will make sure you have a good time, but you must prepare yourself to leave me and this island. You must go home to decide which life you would like to pursue." Carlo walked to her. Standing over her, he looked into the eyes in the mirror over her dressing table coming at him. "No matter what you decide, I will understand and always be here for you."

Soledad didn't weep but stayed dried-eyed. "Will you?" She stood motionless while looking at his reflection in the mirror and waiting for his response.

"I promise you I will. I will, Soledad," he repeated in reassurance. "Do you believe me?"

"I do, and I know you will." Soledad's eyes misted, and she squeezed them shut.

Carlo was pushing her out of his life, and as much as she understood why, she couldn't. Soledad had the taste of Carlo deep inside her, and she couldn't let it go. Soledad wanted to remain with Carlo, sharing his life and bed. She had nothing at home with Elliot but loneliness, misery, and everything with Carlo.

But Carlo was right. She'd have to face her problems at home with Elliot head-on to decide her next step.

Purely as a defensive measure to disengage her emotional gears, Soledad blinked her eyes open and turned to look at Carlo. "Enough of that mushy stuff. I still have many sexless years to make up." She dug out the handcuffs from the drawer and held them up. "Are you joining me in the shower?" Her body language told him she wanted to move on from the conversation, and he obliged.

"Ah, the new Soledad finding her voice. I like her."

"Me too. How about you grab a few goodies from the galley?" Soledad's wink was one of pure mischief. "I'm craving sweets."

"Yes, madam." "Give me fifteen seconds." Carlo's mouth tipped up at one corner.

"Fifteen, fourteen, thirteen...." Counting backward, she crooked a finger at him as she walked away.

Soledad was handcuffed and whipped cream slathered on her. Carlo devoured the strategically placed cherries he set on her body. The whipped cream licked off, he covered her in olive oil and did things to her she imagined Elliot would perceive vulgar and animalistic.

And sweet mercy, Soledad couldn't get enough.

Gliding his fingers between her legs and through the slick, wet heat electrified her, and her body arched and tensed. "Do you like that, *amore*?"

Soledad inhaled deeply, exhaled. "I do. God, I do."

He smiled, appreciating her reaction as much as he enjoyed pleasing her. "I like touching you, Soledad." His mouth was cruising down her neck and shoulders, fogging her head with relentless pleasure.

"I love you touching me."

His fingers on her intensified and flooded her body with need and want. "Does that feel good, Soledad Thomas?" he asked, although her shuddering body spoke volumes.

"Mmm-hmm." Her entire body felt as though it was on fire. "Now, Carlo. Now," she pleaded.

"Look at me, and say my name," he said, seconds before he drove her to the razor-edge and watched her body shudder to orgasm and moaned his name through throaty breaths like a prayer. "I love hearing my name on your lips," he murmured, and breathlessly she cried his name. "Again, Soledad. Say my name again," he urged when he drove her body to quake one last time.

Looking into his eyes, she dug her fingers into his shoulder and repeatedly sang his name as he wanted her to.

She fisted her hands in his hair. "I want you inside me now." Her tone was desperate, demanding.

"Nothing more I'd love." His heart thudding hard in his chest in time with hers, he lifted her hips and thrust himself hard and deep.

Her legs locked around him tightly now. Carlo's hands suspended her as if floating on air as he hammered the final hard drive of himself into her.

Passionately, he sang words in Italian, maybe French, possibly Spanish. She didn't know and didn't care. They all sounded great as he fed her heart with his whispered words and sated her body.

Like a fast-moving wave, she felt him erupt and fill her until he was empty.

"I think my work here is done," he said when he caught his breath.

"Until you're ready to go again," Soledad mused, running a hand over Carlo's wet body.

"Soledad Thomas, you are wearing me out."

"I am, aren't I?" She sent him a proud smile. "I'm craving something salty or savoury now."

"Already. I am going to need ten minutes or so."

She threw back her head and laughed in delight. "I mean food, eggs, toast, maybe some bacon."

"Ah, that type of food. Your wish is my command." He fumbled for the tap and shut the water off. "I'll get breakfast while you throw on your bathing suit. We can go for a swim afterward, and I want to see you in that blue bikini that matches your eyes."

"Alright," she said as easy as Sunday morning.

Chapter 29

CARLO AND SOLEDAD had breakfast on the deck. A glorious beaming sun spilled light from a blue morning sky to beat down on calm water. Terns and seagulls winged over them, and the air carried the smell of sea and brine and rich, wet earth.

"Thank you for this wonderful breakfast." Carlo dipped toast into the yolk of a perfectly cooked sunny-side-up egg, and Soledad mirrored him.

"You know, I didn't even know how to boil eggs when I married. I took a cooking and home economics course when Elliot and I married at the local community center. I wanted to fulfill my wifely duties and make Elliot happy."

"And have you made him happy?" Carlo watched her mull the question over

"I'm not sure," Soledad said after some time.

"Tell me more about your husband."

Soledad looked over at Carlo. The eyes that met hers were clear under the morning light as if they could see through her.

"I was nineteen when Elliot and I met. He was twenty-three and a legacy baby." Soledad explained when confusion filled his eyes. "He was brought into the world to carry his father's name, company, and legacy."

"Ah, something like me."

"Really?

"Certainly. My grandmother, known for enjoying the opposite sex, encouraged me to carry on her legacy. Not to toot my own horn, but I believe I have made her proud." He flashed her a smile that made Soledad's lips curve. "Please go on." Carlo made a rolling hand gesture motioning her to continue.

"I worked as a food server at the university lunchroom, and Elliot walked up to me and asked for a hamburger. Well done, no lettuce or tomato, onions and pickles on one side and ketchup and mustard on the other side of the burger."

"He is a fastidious one." Carlo's expression was somewhere between playful and subdued.

"He is. Along with meticulous, precise, and efficient." She watched Carlo flare a lighter and touch it to the tip of a long, thick reefer.

"He sounds like a party." He inhaled smoke and drew deeply.

A smile played across her face. "He looked bigger than life. He was handsome, in a geeky sort of way, you know. He had big, dark, intelligent eyes behind black-rimmed glasses. I've always been attracted to smart over looks. He was idealistic and ambitious, and he talked to me, a humble food server."

Carlo sighed out the smoke he'd inhaled deep. "There is no shame in having a part-time job, any job, to put yourself through school."

"It wasn't a part-time job to help put me through school. It was one of three jobs I had worked since I was sixteen. My father died of a sudden heart attack then."

Carlo passed the half-smoked spliff to her to uplift the sadness that came over her. Her third puff did the job.

"My father liked to live the high life, and he left a lot of debt behind—more than we ever knew about. I quit school to supplement my mother's meagre cleaner paycheque, to help pay off the debt and support my sister. Christine, my younger sister, had dreamed of studying medicine ever since she was little. She'd worked so hard all of her life, and I didn't want her to give up her dream. I didn't want to break her more than she already was. I didn't want to extinguish her hopes and dreams or contribute to the void my father's passing left in her. She was Daddy's baby girl."

Carlo gestured to a restless Soledad to smoke more to calm her nervous tension, and she did.

"Anyway, after a few weeks of trading pleasantries, Elliot invited me to a frat party. After the shock wore off, I accepted partly because I wanted to get to know him and partly because I wanted to know what the frat thing was about."

Carlo slid a glance at her face. "I do not see you as the animal house type."

Soledad had to laugh. "You'd be right about that. The whole frat scene was so off-putting. Crazy, drunk, immature boys think crossing into manhood is contingent on acting stupid and doing foolish things. But there was a lot of this." Soledad pointed to the joint she took from him. "It helped some. It was the first time I'd tried it." She breathed in smoke.

"Nineteen and a weed virgin, you were a good girl."

Soledad gave his leg a foot nudge. "I was busy working. I didn't have time for fun, let alone clouding my mind and I sure as hell didn't have time for frat nonsense. I started to leave, but Elliot talked me into going…."

"To his place and got down to business," he interjected with a wink.

"You have a one-track mind. Elliot was a perfect gentleman and what he wanted to do was go for a walk. It just so happened the pathway we took led to his apartment."

"My respect for Elliot is back. So you did get down to business."

Her mouth lifted at one corner. "I was a virgin, a sex virgin, and a weed virgin. I wasn't going to put out for just anybody. Anyway, he was agitated, so we smoked more pot."

Carlo's brow winged. "Your Elliot is not so uptight." The munchies kicked in, and Carlo picked up a few slices of toast, slathered them with peanut butter and strawberry jam, and placed a piece in front of her.

"No, he wasn't then. He protested for causes he believed in back then. He was a fighter, an idealist and a dreamer. Anyway, we both got a bit too happy and...."

"You lost your virginity."

"No. We talked without inhibition, and the more I got to know him and his story, the more connected I felt to him. That's when I lost my virginity."

"So, that makes me...."

"My second sexual experience." Soledad finished expecting him to tease her for her very beige life.

Instead, Carlo's glided his lips over hers and said, "I'm flattered to have been chosen."

The action and words made the liquid warmth spread straight to her heart. Now, she took his mouth to give him what beat in her heart. "I...."

"Was he as good as me, Soledad Thomas?" he quipped to stop her from saying what she mustn't. "Please don't tell me he was."

"He was then. I mean, he was my first, and I didn't know better."

Carlo let out a breath. "That was close."

An amused smile brushed over her eyes. "After our second...." She searched for the proper word. "Encounter, Elliot propped himself on his elbow, looked me dead straight, and asked me to marry him."

"The man fell hard fast, but I can see why after our short time together."

Huffing out a breath, Soledad shook her head. "What he fell hard for was my innocence, simplicity, and that I wasn't anything like the women his father steered his way. Elliot was a partier, a trust fund baby with money to burn at his disposal, and his father wanted to put a stop to his carefree way."

"Let me guess. His father threatened to cut Elliot's financial support if he did not marry the woman he handpicked for him, a debutant who spent her days getting her hair bleached platinum-blonde and getting manis and pedis." Carlo shoved the last of his toast in his mouth.

Soledad slid her toast to him when he eyes it. "You know the scenario well."

Carlo nodded. "I have a demanding father who would like to set the roadmap of my life."

"Anyway, marital bliss, by all accounts, tamed the man. So Mr. Thomas believed." Soledad frowned a little. "God, there were a lot of little warning bells back then I didn't pick up."

"There always are, but we do not see them until too late."

"Isn't that the truth? Is there something stronger than coffee?"

"Sure, I will be right back." Carlo went below deck and reappeared with a bottle of scotch. Pouring a shot into her coffee, he handed it to her. Soledad knocked part of the drink back and felt it loosen her stomach. "After the one date, he asks you to marry him? The man does not hammer around."

"I think you mean screw around."

"Yes, that makes more sense," he said after she mimicked the gesture. "You accepted his proposal."

She shook her head. "I liked him, but I didn't love him, and we'd just met. Once the shock wore off, I asked him why he'd propose to someone he barely knew. His response was, 'because I like you and because you're honest and genuine, and beautiful. And because I need to get married in the next few months, or I'll lose my trust fund.'"

"He was honest." Carlo refilled her cup, this time with brandy alone.

Soledad nodded. "Still, I was just nineteen years old. Although all I did was work and didn't have a life, I couldn't tie myself down with a husband and kids. I couldn't bring myself to accept his proposal."

"But you eventually did accept. What made you change your mind?"

She played with her earlobe and wondered what he'd think and say if she told him everything. After a beat of silence, Soledad said, "He offered to pay for my sister's education and financially help my mom. He asked me to give him the son to carry the Thomas legacy in exchange.

I couldn't turn down the offer to ease my mother's work schedule and lift us out of hardship."

He heard the sting of guilt in her voice. "You did what you had to do, Soledad. There is nothing wrong with that, and it does not define you. It is simply one of the many stories in the Soledad Thomas story," he said without hesitation or judgement. "It was a selfless sacrifice you made for the good of your family."

She closed her eyes and scrubbed both hands over her face. "It was for them I did it. I knew what I was getting into when I agreed to marry Elliot. I knew I was getting into an arrangement, not a marriage, and I didn't expect more or demand much. It helped that we got along. I played the doting wife, the perfect host when needed. I kept a clean home, and Elliot was appreciative for all I did for him." Soledad's eyes focused on the vast blue sea gleaming against the sun's reflection.

"For his part, Elliot was kind and caring, attentive. The sex, I assumed, was good. Again, I didn't know better, but it happened often. In time, he grew on me, I fell in love with him, and he told me he fell in love with me. I had problems getting pregnant. It took four years for the doctor to figure it out. So we kept records. We kept track of ovulation time, monthlies, and so on. Sex became clinical, passionless, and predictable. Getting me pregnant was the only outcome of our encounters." Soledad drained part of her brandy to wet her sandpaper dry throat.

"I was thrilled when Hope came, but another part of me was sad. So sad. As much as Elliot loved his daughter, she wasn't the son his father demanded. I felt the same way when Jasmine and the twin girls were born. By then,

I was completely turned off by our sexual encounters, and I sensed Elliot was too, but they had to happen."

"To produce a son," Carlo pointed out, and she nodded.

"After Noah came along, intimacy went by the wayside. I was too tired. Five young children can drain your energy. And frankly, the fire in me was extinguished. There hasn't been intimacy in our marriage for a long, long time. I may be fifty, but I'm not dead." Her eyes sharpened.

"I can vouch for that."

"I still like to ... you know."

"Of course you do."

"I shouldn't have to self-service when a functional man is lying next to me in bed," or feel a void so strong inside me it breaks me.

"No, you should not, Soledad." Carlo's voice rang with understanding.

"A man should see his penis as more than an appendage."

"Pfft, yeah, because what man even does that?"

"Elliot does, that's who. It's not even an attractive appendage. You know."

"I like it," he murmured.

"I mean, a man's naked body is unsightly. Not yours, of course," she corrected when Carlo sent her an arched look.

"Thank you for that."

"Elliot's never home. He's become a workaholic."

"That's not such a bad thing. I mean, look at me." He sat back and stretched his legs, his feet comfortably crossed at the ankles.

"It would be a good thing if he worked for self-fulfillment."

"And he does not?"

Soledad shook her head. "Elliot does it to prove himself to his overly accomplished, overly demanding father who is unpleasable."

"Ah, father and sons."

"You know they say we become our parents, and right or wrong, most of us do our best to defy that rule. Not Elliot. He strives to become his father. His need to become just like him for validation has driven a wedge between us, and his father encourages it." It felt good to say what had been brewing in her for so long.

"No matter how much Elliot does, my father-in-law is never happy, making him work harder, longer hours. He's never home. He's not in the children's lives, my life and his father encourages it." Soledad's eyes cut away from Carlo. "I wasn't the daughter-in-law Charles Winston Thomas wanted, and he's never accepted me." Soledad watched Carlo walk to the rail.

He looked like a painting with a stretch of blue sea and sky as his canvas, his hair windblown, in a sunny-yellow polo shirt, khaki shorts, and tan loafers.

"And you think the old man's been systematically driving a wedge between you for years."

"I do."

Carlo leaned against the rail and crossed his feet at the ankles. Never taking his eyes off her face, he said, "What are you planning to do about it, Soledad?"

Chapter 30

HOPE WOKE UP in her childhood princess bed, in the room she and Jasmine had shared and would always be there for her. That's what Soledad told her daughters.

An oasis of pink, the room looked just as she left it. Pastel pink walls were covered in posters. Hope's side of the room displayed posters of medical women, pioneers in their field, whom she admired: Elizabeth Blackwell, Mary Putnam Jacobi. Jasmine's side had posters of her teen idols Leonardo DiCaprio and Zac Efron, whom she intended to marry, simultaneously. As if.

The desk in front of the picture window overlooking the backyard was neatly organized. That was Hope's doing, not Jasmine's. Jasmine was a slob.

One white dresser with gold trim, two tufted princess beds covered with pink and purple bedspreads and matching pillow shams on plumped pillows. On the nightstand between the beds stood the Barbie lamp Hope and Jasmine fought over many nights.

"Turn it off, Hope," Jasmine screamed.

"I need to study," was Hope's irate response.

"Study at the desk. That's what it's for. I need my beauty sleep." Jasmine aimed lit eyes at her sister.

"Shut up already. I'm more comfortable in bed, and the sooner you shut up, the sooner I can finish."

The banter continued until Jasmine, who always gave in, buried her head under her pillow, and Hope studied until past midnight.

"You passed out last night on the kitchen table, and Daddy carried you to bed." Walking into the bedroom, Jasmine handed Hope the steaming cup of coffee. "Double, double as you like it."

"Thanks. What time is it?" Hope took a sizeable gulp of coffee to give her the kick she needed.

"Ten o'clock."

"Shit, Ethan." With a jolt, Hope sat up straight and reached into her pants pocket for the cell phone.

"Your cell is on the night table. I set it to charge, and Ethan knows you're here. Daddy talked to him last night when he called to see how you were. He's at the hospital. He stayed on to finish off the rest of your shift."

"The man is a saint. He'd just finished a forty-eight-hour shift when he volunteered to take mine over. I don't deserve him." Hope's thoughts on Ethan, she absently sipped hot coffee too quickly and burnt her tongue. An oath-laced rant followed.

Hope was always the most animated of her four siblings, Jasmine thought. "The steam rising from the cup wasn't a giveaway. And you, the brainiac of the Thomas brood."

"Shit, Jasmine, leave them closed." Hope's eyes closed against the sun when Jasmine slid the blind up to let the sun shower bright light into the bedroom.

"Sorry about that." Jasmine wound the blind higher to let more sun spill into the room.

"You always were a shithead."

Jasmine's grin flashed wide. "That would be me. Annie and Allie are making breakfast if you're hungry."

"Has no one informed them that pouring milk over cereal is not making breakfast?"

"You're preaching to the wrong choir. Unlike you, I'm not a perfectionist and can overlook people's deficiencies. I'm more of a live-and-let-live kind of girl."

"Right." Hope propped her back against the tufted headboard. "Have we heard from the cops?"

"No, and I'm not so sure we'll get much help from them." Jasmine turned to make her bed she'd left unmade so as not to wake Hope. "They don't suspect foul play and believe Mom left of her own accord." She smoothed out the bedspread and propped the pillow against the headboard before taking a seat at the edge of the bed.

Hope studied her sister over the rim of her coffee cup. "You don't look worried or concerned."

"I was at first, but the more I think about it…." Jasmine paused.

Hope stopped her coffee drinking mid-sip. "Spit it out. What's that hamster in your head whispering?"

"That never gets old for you, does it?" Jasmine said and made her sister snort a giggle. "Anyway, after giving it some thought, I figure Mom just stepped off for a bit. You know, to get some time for herself and do something she wants while getting our attention."

"Without telling a soul? I don't know." Hope stretched out her legs.

"That's exactly how she'd get our attention. Think about it. She has no friends or anyone to talk to, not that she'd talk to us about her grownup issues. The point is she has no one to talk to. Dad's never home and neither are we anymore. The twins and Noah are young and in the all-about-me phase. Aunt Christine, her only friend, is far away, leading this exciting life with her gorgeous husband while Mom's at home cooking, cleaning, running errands, and...."

"Living the dream, I get it." Hope set her cup down and walked to the dresser. Looking at her reflection in the round mirror above the dresser, she cringed at what she saw. She tamped the frizzed mass of dark-colored hair with a brush, ran fingers under her shadowed eyes to stimulate circulation, and pinched her pale cheeks to put a trace of colour. "It's one of the reasons I've turned down Ethan's proposal—twice."

Jasmine's eyes went wide, and her mouth rounded. "You never said, and why wouldn't you accept? I mean, he adores you. Why he does, is a mystery to us all, but he does?"

"I'm that good in bed." Hope quipped.

"You handle carbolic acid in that hospital of yours?"

Hope whirled to face Jasmine. "Not me personally, but yeah, why?"

"I need it to scrub the mental picture you just put in my brain."

Hope snorted a laugh. "I hate to say it, but I don't want to end up like Mom. I don't want the type of humdrum life Mom leads. I want the excitement of Auntie Christine's, and tying myself down won't allow it. Ethan wants a home and children."

"You don't."

"I do, and I love Ethan, but I also want more. Tying myself down with a husband and children won't permit me to pursue my dreams. Don't ever buy into the hype that a woman can do it all, have it all because we can't.

Life's limitations are more amplified for women than for men. It's either this or that for us."

"You've always been a party, Hope."

"I've always been a realist."

"You tell yourself that."

"You know Mom wanted to become a dancer. She never told us for fear we'd feel as if we're the reason for her dashed dreams. At least that's what Auntie Christine told me. Auntie Christine told me Mom took ballet until she was sixteen when Grandpa died and had to give it up for work. Her dream died when she started having us, and Daddy wouldn't get her help because Grandfather would disapprove."

"'A Thomas stands on their own two feet no matter the challenge.'" Jasmine mimicked Charles's surly voice.

"Grandfather, the Genghis Khan of our times." Hope got to her feet. "I need to get out of these scrubs."

"Grandfather's not so bad." Jasmine watched Hope walk to the closet stocked with Polo shirts and jeans from their teen years.

"I know you know that's not true, or maybe you refused to see beyond the dollar signs in your eyes. You're laying the groundwork for Grandfather's will to sway in your favour." Hope chose an orange shirt, faded jeans, and hoped they still fit.

"That's not true," said Jasmine defiantly.

"That high-pitched, defensive tone right there tells me I'm right," Hope lobbed back, and Jasmine thought better than to start the argument she'd lose. Aside from Soledad, no one knew Jasmine better than Hope. "You'd better be prepared to give Grandfather blood, sweat, and tears. I love Grandfather, he's blood, but he didn't get where he is by being compassionate. Didn't you tell me you're interviewing to replace his fifth assistant in four years?"

"Fourth in five years." Jasmine corrected.

"Sorry, because that makes it better. He's never treated Mom like family." Hope slipped her hand into the top dresser drawer and fished for underwear and a bra. It was years since she'd moved out, yet everything was in its place, recently washed, and smelled of Downy. That was Soledad's way.

"I know you've seen how Grandfather dismisses Mom. Worse than the dismissal is the fact Daddy allows it and never stands up for her. As much as I love Daddy, that's something I can't forgive him for, and as much as I love Mom, I have little respect for her for allowing it. Her leaving has restored my respect for her. It's about damn time Mom showed Daddy she's her own woman." Hope disappeared into the bathroom, leaving Jasmine mulling that over.

Chapter 31

Sixty Hours Later

ON THE DECK of The Xanadu, Soledad tasted salt, sea, and man. The years of repressed fantasies and need ripped through her, and she took all she could from him.

The sensation along her skin where his fingertips explored the curve of her body and breasts was pure fire. His teeth scraped along her jaw before his mouth took hers, hot and hard.

Carlo made Soledad's blood hum as he drove into her harder, faster. Her heart galloped in her chest to the beat of their untamed lovemaking. Soledad threw her head back, closed her eyes, and let out quiet, throaty moans that echoed in his ears.

Her hands clutched at his hair, her legs tightened around his hips, and she rose and fell with him in orchestrated rhythm. She held on tight to him, hot, damp flesh, pounding against flesh as if never wanting to let him go. Floating in the synchronized dance that was theirs, he drove the shock of heat into her and she into him.

She wanted everything he was inside her.

Her breath caught and released on a sigh as her body strained and rode the orgasm with him.

"Once again, a solid ten, Soledad Thomas." Carlo opened his arms, and Soledad leaned into him, her face snug against his chest.

"I never thought of myself as a ten, in any way," she said, breathing in his scent.

"Well, you are that and more in every way." Carlo tilted his eyes up and kept them level on her. "I have told you. I speak only the truth to you."

"Thank you for taking me scuba diving."

Scuba diving after breakfast, something Soledad always wanted to try but never had, was what Carlo promised and delivered. The wonder of underwater life was a wondrous experience she regretted not doing sooner.

The splendid coral reef she saw through goggled eyes and the sea life it was home to was something she would never forget. Fish, including a drifting shark and gray stingray, the sea turtle that lazily swam around the underwater field of tall, feathery plumes of seaweed swaying with the ocean, dazzled her. She was glad she'd finally taken the plunge and did it. Had Elliot been there, he would have talked her out.

"It's too dangerous. You're too old to try something as challenging as scuba diving. You'll hurt yourself or worse," Elliot would say to dissuade Soledad.

Once upon a time, Elliot was the adventurous man Carlo was. The adventure left Elliot long ago.

Carlo ran a hand over Soledad's hair. "I am happy you enjoyed our excursion below water."

"I did, very much. It gave me time to think."

"What about, my love?"

"The children, Elliot, the life I've left behind, and you." Soledad glanced over at Carlo. His hair was tousled, and his powerful shoulders and hard chest gleamed under the bright sun with a light sheen of sweat. She could smell the muskiness of man.

How could she give the adventurous, electrifying Carlo up for cautious, dull Elliot? How could she go back to her lacklustre life after tasting the exhilarating life and electrifying sex Carlo introduced to her?

Soledad fell into a contemplative silence. For a long while, she said nothing as she turned thoughts in her head.

Soledad didn't want the happiness and fulfillment she found with Carlo to end, but he was right. She had a decision to make, return to her family or remain with Carlo on Topaz Island.

Their eyes met. Carlo's eyes were as black as the darkest night. She adored looking into them when she woke next to him and made love. Soledad wanted to look into his eyes for the rest of her life.

In a moment of complete understanding, he said, "You must go back to your life, Soledad."

"I don't want to. I could stay here with you forever." A tear spilled over and tracked a line down her cheek.

"But you must go back."

Soledad nodded. "I know, and I will, but not because of Elliot, but for my children."

Carlo took her hand and toyed with her fingers. "You don't have to explain."

She did. "An affair is not the example I want to set for my children." The feeling of abject loneliness and emptiness she already felt at the thought of leaving him made the tears swell in her eyes.

"I understand."

"Do you?" Her eyes swam when she lifted them to his face.

"I do, *amore*, and you must forget me. I am but a passing ship in the night." Soledad understood Carlo had taken the first step away from her in that instant.

"I can't. I won't."

He touched her, just his fingertips on her cheek, to smooth away the pain he saw in her eyes.

"You can and you will because you go back stronger and wiser, Soledad Thomas. You have found your voice, and you will no longer live with the unspoken understanding of your obsoleteness. You will demand to be seen and heard by Elliot and everyone in your life. It is now written you will live the life *you* deserve. Swear to me you will be your own woman, Soledad Thomas." Carlo's tone and eyes radiated so much love it gave her the strength to understand what he said, and Soledad nodded.

Carlo stepped off the boat and held out a hand. After the briefest of hesitations, her hand reached out for his. "You are no longer cast adrift, Soledad, and you are loved," he said with that beautiful smile she would never forget.

Chapter 32

"MOM, WE'RE HOME." Noah dropped his equipment bag on the foyer and bent down to give Buddy a head scratch when he ran up to greet him. "Did you see how I clapped that last goal into the net?" Noah swung the imaginary hockey stick, reliving the moment.

"It was a great move, bud. You caught Dad's eye and a prouder grandfather he couldn't be. And ditto for me." Elliot closed the front door and dropped his key on the console table. "Soledad, come congratulate your hockey-star son on the great game he played." Elliot shrugged out of his jacket, and Noah followed suit.

"I'm going to wash up." Noah picked his jacket off the floor when Elliot handed him the hanger and hung it in the closet.

"Don't take too long. We leave in half an hour. Text your sisters to get their butts home now. They can continue their flirting with your teammates at a later date." Elliot loosened his tie and unbuttoned the top two on his shirt. "Soledad, where the hell are you?" Elliot called out again.

Elliot's voice roused Soledad. Dragging herself out of the dream, she opened her eyes to the shapes and shadows of the dark room. Hazy and disoriented, Soledad sat up in bed and studied her surroundings. She was in her bedroom, on the bed she shared with Elliot, not Carlo.

Soledad's eyes came into focus. She saw the black dresser with the vertical silver handles and the family portrait hanging on the wall above it. Looking to her right, she caught sight of the arched table lamp. Continuing her scan of the room, Soledad's eyes landed on the picture window with a view of her backyard.

Soledad was in her house on Topaz Crescent. She was far away from Topaz Island, Carlo, and his yacht.

Brushing hands over her face, Soledad heard Elliot and Noah's voices flow from the foyer to her room, and things became clearer. She remembered falling asleep after her shower that afternoon. Carlo, Topaz Island, and The Xanadu existed in her imagination. In that instant, the line between fantasy and reality wore down. The strong, confident Soledad who had found her voice was a figment of her imagination. She didn't exist.

Wiping the sleep out of her eyes, Soledad turned to the clock radio on the night table and saw the bright 7:00. She'd been asleep for five hours. "Shit, I didn't make dinner." Soledad jumped to her feet and shrugged into jeans and a baggy sweatshirt.

"Here you are," Elliot said, opening the bedroom door. "We've been calling for you."

"I'm sorry. I fell asleep." Shadowed in the room's darkness, with the hallway light eclipsing him, Soledad thought she saw Carlo. "Is that you?"

"Of course, it's me."

The voice that came at her was Elliot's, but it sounded so much like Carlo's. The line between imagination and reality had become too thin to define.

"Who else would it be?" Elliot flipped the lights on, walked up to Soledad, and caught sight of her red-rimmed eyes. "Are you all right, Soledad?"

She turned to give him her back when she felt the weight of his gaze on her. "Yes. Yes, I'm fine."

"Look at me, Soledad." Elliot skimmed a glance over Soledad's face when she turned to him.

"I need to get dinner started."

"No, don't bother. My father invited us to Maxim's to celebrate Noah's win tonight. Have you been crying, Soledad?" Elliot's tone was that of a man disarmed by a woman's tears.

"I'm surprised you noticed."

Elliot's eyes stayed on Soledad as she walked away from him toward the bathroom. She was in one of her moods—again. He usually left her to brood when she got like this, but something tugged at Elliot, and he followed her.

Arched in the doorway, Elliot watched Soledad dab water on her face. "Why have you been crying, Soledad?"

Soledad whirled to face him and stared. Water dripped from her face onto the floor tile. Had she become so insignificant that he still didn't remember she had crossed a milestone twenty-four hours ago?

She snagged the towel from the towel bar and dried her face. "It's nothing."

Elliot shut his eyes and pressed his fingers to them. "Christ, Soledad, I can't read your mind. Just tell me what's bothering you."

Her first impulse was to spring to attack, but her sadness was too heavy and stole her voice. She didn't speak, and as he always did, Elliot turned to walk away.

"We don't even argue anymore," she murmured.

Elliot sighed. "What are you talking about, Soledad?"

"You don't even care enough to argue with me." Her thin shoulders hunched over.

Elliot shut the bedroom door. "You want to fight, is that it?"

"It would be something. It would show you cared, that you were passionate about us, about our life."

"What the hell are you talking about, Soledad." He reached into the drawer for the cashmere V-neck. "Change into something decent. You know you can't wear jeans to Maxim's."

"You mean your father doesn't like us to wear jeans. It's too pedestrian." Her stomach roiled with nerves, but she pressed on. "I'm not changing, and I'm not going to Maxim's, and neither is Noah. It's a pretentious restaurant for stuffy old men, not a sixteen-year-old boy. Noah hates it there. I hate it. You hate it." She felt the power of her voice, heard it. "We're going to Marcello's Pizzeria." Her voice was firm.

Elliot hadn't heard or seen the Soledad before him, and he stared dully.

"You heard right, Elliot. I'm saying what I should have said long ago." That hard line between what was and what is was waning. "Tell your father he's welcome to join us for dinner. Change into something more comfortable and be ready to leave in fifteen minutes," she said, walking out of the bedroom and leaving an open-mouthed Elliot staring after her.

She had found her voice and would no longer live with the unspoken understanding of her obsoleteness.

Chapter 33

MARCELLO'S WAS THICK with post-game diners. Hockey players and their parents, family, and fans celebrated the big win against the rival Flash Lightning. The air was ripe with the rich scents of garlic, tomato sauce, and baking pizza. From behind the counter, Marcello's boisterous voice called out for order pick-up over the chatter of excited teenagers weighing in their view of the game. The Weeknd's *I Feel It Coming* drifted from the overhead speakers.

The Thomas's easily managed to get a booth in the crowded restaurant since Marcello was a fan of The Devils and its captain Noah.

From the moment they walked into Marcello's Pizzeria, the twins, like a tornado, wound their way from table to table. Soledad and Elliot stopped at tables or waved their hellos to parents and Noah's teammates on their way to their table. Seated at their booth, Soledad ordered two large pizzas loaded with pepperoni, as Noah liked and a vegetarian for the twins. She ordered spicy chicken wings with blue cheese dip for Elliot and Noah and a Caesar salad for her. With the food, Soledad ordered a glass of Zinfandel for herself and netted her a stunned, lingering look from Elliot.

Schoolmates stopped at the table to congratulate Noah on his performance, and fellow hockey players high-fived him in passing. Girls gave Noah the sultry, admiring looks Soledad feared would have him crossing into manhood sooner than she hoped.

Soledad thought there were so many reasons her children deserved to be at their local hangout and not at some uppity restaurant. Elliot would never admit it to Soledad, but she knew he too believed so.

Youth was for having fun, spending time with friends, and doing silly teenage things. Although her children's life would never be as difficult a journey as hers had been, it would nonetheless bring on the challenges of adulthood. Soledad wouldn't fast-track them into adulthood, not as she had been forced to.

Soledad signalled for another Zinfandel when Elliot waved the waiter over to order another beer. Progress, Soledad thought when Elliot didn't stop her from ordering or made a snide remark about drinking too much.

"Absorb all this happiness, Elliot." Soledad studied him as she took a long sip of her wine. He'd shed the designer suit, silk tie, and the loafers for a comfortable pair of jeans and a sweatshirt that read U of T—his alma mater. "Your children are having a great time, and your son is a star in every girl's eye. Isn't that every father's dream?" Soledad watched Noah's grin as Marci and Monica scooped him away from the table.

"Yeah, well, Dad wasn't pleased with the dinner cancellation." Elliot took a pull of his beer.

The smirk twisted her lips. "But our children are happy, and that's worth more to me than pleasing your unreasonably demanding father."

Elliot gave Soledad a stupefied look. "What's gotten into you, Soledad? Drinking and disrespecting the hand that feeds you."

"By that, do you mean you or your father? Don't bother to answer because you don't know either." Soledad went silent as the waiter approached the table to set fresh beer and wine on the table and scooped up the empties. When they were alone again, she continued. "I've earned my way. You're surprised I'm showing I have a backbone, Elliot. Frankly, I am too, and I like it. So, get used to it because it's here to stay."

Elliot looked at her. Aside from being shocked by her clipped response, Elliot was impressed by her. "Okay, if you say so."

"I do." Soledad was civil to him now, but the chill radiating from her was palpable.

He'd wracked his brain and still hadn't come up with what had triggered Soledad's angry outburst. And for the life of him, Elliot had even less of a clue as to what had turned Soledad into the biting woman before him. No matter how long he lived, he'd never understand women. Venus was the right place for them.

"How is work?" Soledad drank some of her wine.

The voice that punched like a fist seconds ago flowed musically now, and Elliot thought Venus was the right place for women. "It's work," Elliot said, giving Soledad the miserable expression that came over him when he spoke of work.

"I'm sorry, Elliot."

"About what?" Elliot took another pull of his beer.

She looked right at him. "Your misery, the sadness that fills you because of your work. It can't be a pleasant feeling." Soledad watched Elliot absently pick at the label on his beer bottle. "It's changed you, Elliot."

"All of a sudden, you've become a psychoanalyst."

"You're no longer the caring, loving man I married. You put your job, a miserable one at that, ahead of your family and me."

Elliot gave Soledad a disinterested look. "Not this again, Soledad. This is getting old."

"Not to me, Elliot. I want my husband back, and I need to be more than your maid and cook." Soledad spoke calmly, her eyes solemn.

Elliot's eyes went hard. "Christ, Soledad, you're none of those things. You're my wife."

"It hasn't felt that way for a long time, Elliot."

"I work my fingers to the bone to provide for you and the children. You live in a beautiful home and drive a nice car, and we'll soon have three children in university simultaneously. Do you know what that costs?"

"I do, but we'll manage like every other family."

"Spoken like a woman who hasn't worked a day and has been handed everything to her." Elliot took a calming breath. "I'm sorry, I didn't mean that."

Her eyes calm and level on his, she said, "On the contrary. You meant every word, but I'm going to let it slide. The old Soledad wouldn't, but the new Soledad feels sorry for you, Elliot."

"Well, don't. I don't need your pity." Elliot waved the waiter over to the table and ordered a double scotch. Hard liquor was what he needed now.

"Why don't you start your own accounting firm? It'll get you out from under your father's thumb and give you back your life."

"Because he likes it where he is," Charles Winston Thomas's imperious voice came at Soledad from over her shoulder. "Classy place," he said with a cocked brow as his dark eyes circled the restaurant.

The new Soledad wouldn't allow Charles to make her feel inadequate. "You've always wanted Elliot to prove himself, Charles, and what better way to do it than starting his firm. You're not afraid of the competition, are you?" If the sudden shock of her unexpected bold remark surprised Charles, it didn't register on his face.

"Stop it, Soledad. Sit down, Dad. Good of you to join us."

Charles took the seat Elliot vacated. At seventy-four, Charles had a thick shock of silver hair, and his face was handsomely etched with the roadmap of his successful life. He wore a black Savile Row suit and a soft-blue silk shirt and tie, which screamed affluence in the quaint restaurant, but that was precisely the message he wanted to telegraph to everyone in the restaurant.

"Competition, from Elliot? Elliot wouldn't know where to begin if he went on his own. He'd be a fish out of the water if he left the cushy, well-paying job he has with me?" The haughty grin showed perfect, white teeth against the spray-tanned face.

The woman who would have recoiled into herself didn't exist anymore. The new Soledad who wanted to slap the smug expression on Charles's face did and said what she'd wanted to say for some time. "You're scared of going up against Elliot. It's why you've boxed him in and kept him under your thumb all these years. Your son, Charles." Soledad was happy when she got Elliot's full attention.

"Hmmm," was Charles's stunned response, and because his temper was starting to spike, he followed it with, "You should learn to reign in your deluded wife, Elliot, and get me a drink. Now, Elliot."

"Yes, yes, of course, Father." Elliot raised his glass and signalled to the waiter to bring two more. He was going to need the infusion of alcohol as much as his father did.

Soledad wished Elliot would grow a spine. Until he did, she'd stand up for herself and him. She would no longer allow Charles to make her feel as inadequate and irrelevant as he aimed to.

Soledad looked at Charles with defiant eyes. "Stop being so overbearing, Charles. It will not work with me anymore, and it will no longer work on Elliot." And in another first, Soledad said, "Your poor wife endured your bullshit for years, but I will not."

That struck Charles hard. "You leave Lizzie out of this."

"I was boxed in, and I couldn't help that dear woman, but I will help my family now," Soledad finished.

Charles's dark eyes, hot with anger, turned to Elliot. "Are you going to allow your wife to disrespect your mother and me?"

"Please keep your voices down. We are in a restaurant," Elliot pointed out while scanning the room for his children and spotted the twins five tables down in lively conversation and Noah, one table over, being dazzled by a curvy blonde. That would keep them occupied long enough to avoid witnessing world war three erupting at the table.

"Elliot will permit me—as you archaically put it—to speak if he knows what's good for him." Soledad's tone was lined with steel.

Charles's jaw set tightly. "You have always been a gutless wonder, son."

"As I was saying, Charles, I've suspected your obnoxious behaviour toward your son stems from the fear of Elliot outshining the great Charles Winston Thomas. Lately, however, your irrelevancy has turned that obnoxiousness into right-down cruelty. Modernization and computerization are making an old man obsolete. I can appreciate your fear of getting old. I don't appreciate you taking your anger out on my family, Jasmine and Elliot."

With a dash of exhilaration and a dab of fear, a little thrill fluttered inside Elliot as he watched, with delight and envy, the woman who looked like his wife take on his father like a bull charging its toreador.

"Christ, Elliot, grow a backbone and deal with your woman." Face fierce, Charles picked up the glass the waiter set before him and drained it. "Bring the bottle. Now," he barked at the server.

"Sir, we don't sell bottles." Eighteen-year-old, pimpled-face Bobby informed.

"I said now." The scorching look Charles gave Bobby sent him scarpering from the table.

"I'm not *his* woman, Charles, and we don't need your money."

"Soledad, three kids in university," Elliot murmured between clenched teeth.

"Listen to your husband." Charles's eyes were hard as stone.

"I may not be a Chartered Accountant or an educated woman, but I was always good with money. Growing up poor is an education in money management. So, as the family's money manager, I've saved and wisely invested our savings." Soledad looked Elliot in the eyes. "We're sitting on a small fortune. Enough capital to launch your firm, Elliot, hire Jasmine to help you put it together, a couple of accountants to start, and still leave a nice retirement fund."

Elliot aimed a dumbfounded look at her. "Jesus, Soledad. How much money do we have?"

"Last I checked, Edward, our financial advisor, told me the total sum in our combined accounts was three million five hundred and sixty-eight thousand two hundred and fifty dollars and twenty-five cents."

Eyes fixed wide in shock, Elliot stared at Soledad. "We have a financial advisor?"

"We do, and I think you should hire him when you're ready. He has a brilliant mind for investing."

The shock still glazing Elliot's eyes, he said, "Christ on a bike, I'd say so, and how did I not know about this?"

"You're always too busy, and I took it upon myself to take care of the investing and finances and the yearly taxes," Soledad said, and the guilt hit Elliot like a freight truck.

Charles's face, set in serious lines, hissed. "Need I remind you where that money came from?"

"It came from…."

"Let me, Soledad." With the newfound strength injected into him by the woman twice the man he was, Elliot found his voice. "It came from my hard work, Dad. It came from the twelve to fourteen hour, seven-day weeks you have me working. It came from forgoing my family and wife to secure your bottom line. It came from your greedy demands and extraordinary need to control my life. Soledad is right, Dad. You drove Mom to her grave. You put those same demands on her, and she couldn't take it anymore," Elliot said, surprising himself and feeling a strange sense of relief at finally saying the words he had wanted to say for so long. "God, that felt good."

Charles's face filled with angry red. "Careful, Elliot, have you forgotten whom you're speaking to?"

"No, Dad, I haven't, and you are speaking to the president of Stuart & Partners."

Soledad swept a blue gaze over Elliot. "It's your company, Elliot. I don't need my maiden name on the billing, and you should be the C.E.O."

"You do, and you will be the C.E.O. After all, you're my partner in every sense."

Soledad and Elliot's eyes locked. In a moment of recognition, Soledad saw the man she married looking back at her for the first time in years. She blinked at the tears.

"This is all very touching, but you're not going anywhere, Elliot. You have a contract with me." Charles put in.

"Your father made you sign a contract?"

Elliot nodded. "Every two years, but it's up to him to hold me to it and give me access to all his business information for another ten months, which is when it expires."

Defeat leaving a bad taste in Charles's mouth, he rose to his feet and gave Soledad and Elliot a snide stare before storming out of the restaurant.

Chapter 34

"WAS THAT GRANDFATHER's town car I saw pulling out of the parking lot?" Jasmine asked when she walked up to the booth.

"It was." Elliot sipped on his third beer of the night.

"He said he'd wait." Jasmine shook out of her jacket as Bobby sprinted to her side.

"Hey, Jasmine, you looked great tonight. I mean professionally great. That suit...." Bobby's words became tangled when he felt Elliot's eyes on him.

"Hey, Bobby, you're looking studly tonight," Jasmine said, putting a smile on the teen boy's face who'd stumbled into love with her and lived in hope. After ordering a round of drinks and whispering into Bobby's ear, Jasmine watched him set off with a skip and a smile.

"You shouldn't tease the boy, Jasmine," Soledad said.

"It put a smile on his face, didn't it?" Jasmine slid into the booth next to her mother. "Where are Noah and the twins?"

"They're making the rounds." Soledad tilted her chin toward them.

"So, is Grandfather coming back?" Jasmine reached for a slice of pizza.

"No, he, um, got called away." Elliot sipped beer to quench the lie.

"He's probably pissed I'm late, but we ... I mean, I took longer than I thought, but at this time, it's not easy to…. Never mind." Jasmine picked up Soledad's drink and sipped. "Mom, this is alcohol." She swallowed some more. "Zinfandel, to be exact. So not like you." Jasmine tossed the rest of the drink back.

"And so like you to identify the drink on a couple of sips," Elliot said.

"Yeah, well, you know." Jasmine breathed a sigh of relief when Hope and Ethan walked into the restaurant and sidetracked the conversation. "Look who's here, Mom."

Soledad beamed a smile. "It's so nice to see you both." She slid out of the booth to hug Hope and Ethan tight.

Soledad thought of a youthful Elliot, looking at the young man she considered a part of her family.

Ethan was inches taller than Hope with intelligent hazel-coloured eyes. His short hair, a tawny shade of brown, was damp from his shower. Like Hope, Ethan wore jeans torn at the knees, a hoodie, and running shoes because downplaying the brilliant heart surgeon he was becoming was who he was.

"Nice to see you, Mrs. T., Mr. T." Ethan pumped Elliot's hand and then hung Hope's and his jacket on the coat rack next to the booth.

"You kids hungry?" Soledad slid close to Elliot to make seating room for Hope and Ethan.

"I'm starving."

"Me too," Ethan echoed Hope.

"Honey, order another pizza, some more chicken wings, a couple of panzerotti, and salads for the kids from Marcello at the counter. We'll get it faster," Soledad said to Elliot.

"Sure, honey. I'll be right back." Elliot's peck on Soledad's cheek drew bewildered stares from Hope and Jasmine. "What's with the gawking?"

Hope and Jasmine gave their father a long, silent look.

"Is everything all right, Mom?" Hope said when her father walked away. "Are you okay?" She brought a hand to her mother's forehead.

Soledad had to smile at the idea that a shared tender moment between her and Elliot raised concerns in her daughter. "Everything's fine, honey, perfectly fine."

"Hope, Jasmine, and Ethan are here," Allie called out to Annie and leaned in to hug everyone.

Annie followed with, "Sup, siblings? Hey, Future-brother-in-law," before she turned her attention to her screen's phone.

"Sup, Ethan? Thought you'd dump her bossy ass by now." Noah gave chuckling Ethan a fist bump while Hope sent him a slitted look. "Bobby told me to come to join you. What's up?" Noah's attention was distracted by the ping of an incoming text.

"Shut up, all of you. Put those phones away, and sit down," Jasmine ordered.

"Do you ever get tired of telling people what to do? You know I'm the MVP of the night."

"Shut up and sit, Noah." Jasmine's eyes flashed up at Noah like two flares.

With a hissed breath, Noah sat and quickly sidestepped his irritation at his sister when Bobby set the food on the table. "Thanks, Bobby, you read my mind. I'm starving." Noah grabbed a chicken wing from the basket and made a low sound of pleasure.

Annie shook her head. "You're like a trash compactor, Noah. You just finished eating a basket of wings at Marci's table."

"Ah, no. It's been a half-hour. Ethan, you're a doctor. Explain to my idiot sister how much food a hockey star needs to intake."

Hope held up a hand to cut Ethan off when he started to speak. "Don't dignify that with a response."

"Yeah, don't elevate him to human grade. Exhibit A." Annie pointed to Noah's sauced-stained mouth and fingers.

Soledad didn't stop the bickering. Her children were headstrong individuals, and she'd given up hoping for the Beaver Cleaver family long ago. The bickering, name-calling, insulting children were who they were, and she relished the moment. To have all her children together around the table sharing a meal warmed her heart.

Minutes later, Bobby carrying a cake with sparkles flaring—as Jasmine instructed—and the waiters trailing him walked up to the booth singing happy birthday. Soon after, everyone in the restaurant joined in wishing Soledad a happy birthday.

The surprise on Soledad's face was swift and the smile wide.

Elliot felt a prick of conscience when he recognized his enormous mistake. He forgot Soledad's birthday. After thirty-one years of marriage, he forgot his wife's fiftieth, a milestone in anyone's life.

Thinking back to the past Monday, the day of Soledad's birthday, his father kept him busy until late reviewing the Wingate account for the upcoming Wednesday meeting. Having dedicated much of his time working the account in the past year, Elliot didn't give it a second thought. Ryan Wingate's decision to turn over the financial management of his multi-national restaurant chain would elevate Thomas and Partners to international status.

Elliot realized now his father purposely held him back and that Soledad was right. His father was a vindictive, petty man. Cursing under his breath, Elliot looked over at Soledad, but before he could say anything, Hope cut him off.

"I'm sorry we forgot your birthday, Mom." Hope pecked Soledad on the cheek. "It came to me today after work, and I called Jasmine right away."

"It's why I was so late. I had to go to three bakeries in search of your favourite cake." Jasmine cut eight slices of red velvet covered in cream cheese frosting and set them on the plates Bobby brought.

"We're sorry too, Mom," The twins said, and Noah followed with his apology through a mouthful of cake.

"Better late than never, I say, and having my family around me makes it the perfect birthday." Soledad's smile spread cheek to cheek.

Eyes mirroring remorse and shame, Elliot lay a hand on Soledad's and linked his fingers with hers. "I, too, am very sorry I forgot your birthday, Soledad."

Elliot was a man who'd lost his way and taken her for granted, but he was the man who completed her and made her whole. Soledad was sure he'd find a way to put everything right again.

Soledad squeezed Elliot's hand. That simple act told him everything would be right between them again.

Chapter 35

SOLEDAD LOOKED OVER at Elliot. He looked Handsome, confident, and relaxed, so very relaxed. His eyes were shaded behind a pair of aviator glasses. He wore khakis, a crisp moss-green Polo shirt tucked into them, and tan loafers. The staggeringly blue sky and shimmering diamond sea canvassed him. A pair of gulls dove into the salty water. After a few seconds, they surfaced with fish in beaks and winged to land.

The captain of the yacht set sail, and Elliot's dark hair flitted in the air. At that moment, Elliot looked like Carlo from her dream.

When the sweet smell of her perfume flowed into him, Elliot looked up to meet Soledad's blue gaze. She wore a fuchsia bikini. The flowery sarong tied at her waist floated in the air in concert with the chestnut hair that spilled down to her suntanned shoulders.

"You look great," Elliot said, closing the distance between them.

"Back at you." Soledad played her mouth over his. "I had a great time last night."

Sex had never been stormy between them, downright dull most times. Last night, however, the ocean lashed under the light of a full moon and a star-lit night, and thunder boomed. The fact they made love floating on the joint they'd shared before they grappled each other like rabid animals or that the crew asleep below deck might catch them injected a thrilling element to their lovemaking.

"Me too." He combed his fingers through her hair.

"You brought out the best in me. I didn't know I was that good."

She skimmed a finger over his cheek. "Well, I can assure you that you were."

His smile and ego swelled. "This trip was a great idea, and it's the perfect way to recharge before I set our new venture in motion. Stuart & Partners does have a nice ring to it."

"It does, but as I said before, I'm perfectly fine with only your name on the marquis. I don't need the recognition."

"You deserve the credit more so than I do. You're the reason for the adventure we're about to embark on." Elliot walked to the teak table with the chef's breakfast spread of omelettes, fried plantain, black beans, and empanadas. Picking up the flutes of mimosas, he handed one to Soledad.

"Well, I don't doubt that the company will be a great success with you and Jasmine as your right-hand person." Crystal rang against crystal as Soledad tapped her glass to his.

"I don't doubt it. Jasmine's smart, hard-working, and beautiful. She's very much like her mother."

The flush of pink rose to Soledad's cheeks. Elliot had always found her modesty an alluring trait. It was what drew him to the girl with the flyaway hair and red cheeks behind the lunch counter. Soledad was natural and genuine, unlike the women his father had steered in his direction.

"It won't hurt that Mr. Wingate refused to do business with anyone other than you and signed on with you and not your father's firm." She watched Elliot turn contemplative as he sipped on his drink. "Stop feeling guilty, Elliot. You insisted to Mr. Wingate he sign on with your father."

"I did, but…."

"It was his choice, Elliot. He knew who the better man for the job was. Mr. Wingate seems to me like the type of man who knows his mind. You deserve this, Elliot. We deserve this. You're finally your own boss. You can set your hours and be home more often for the children. For me."

"There will be some travelling. It is an international account," Elliot pointed out.

"Jasmine's young, energetic, and adventurous."

"That she is," Elliot agreed.

"She can take on some of the travelling until I staff the company. I think, though, when it comes to those romantic, exotic locales, the two senior partners, as in you and I, should step in."

"You've put some thought into this."

Soledad smiled over the rim of her flute. "I've had a lot of time to think about many things."

"I know, and I'm sorry."

Soledad's eyes met Elliot's in a moment of recognition and complete understanding. "I know you are."

He slid his fingers under her chin. "You, Soledad, are the best thing to happen to me and will forever be among the best choices I've made. You are the best of me, and I love who I am when I'm with you."

Soledad saw the love in his eyes. No longer would Soledad Thomas fade into the background, she thought.

"What do you want for yourself, Soledad? You loved ballet."

"I think that ship's sailed." There was no resentment in Soledad's voice, remorse, anger, or self-pity.

Elliot's stomach knotted with guilt. He glanced sideways, then away. "I'm sorry I kept you from fulfilling your dream."

Soledad held up a hand to his cheek. "You didn't. I traded up. You and the children are everything to me. I'll find my way. I always have. For now, I want us to spend time together. We have a lot of catching up to do."

He smiled. "I'm yours forever now. I do love you, Soledad, and always will."

"I love you too, Elliot, and I always will." Soledad rested her head on the shoulder, which would now always be there for her.

There was no past anymore. There was only the now.

Sneak peek at M.L. Lexi's new novel

THE GRIEVING WOMAN

One

Fall 2002

TODAY WAS THE day.

For weeks, Coco plotted, planned, and lied to make today happen. Now that the day was here, she was regretting it. There are doors that, once opened, can't be closed again.

Tapping the cell phone alarm off, Coco rubbed exhaustion out of her eyes. She hadn't had a decent night's sleep in weeks, and last night was no exception. Sitting up in bed, Coco brought her knees up, pressed her face into them and took a moment to gather her thoughts. As much as she'd mentally prepared for today, she wasn't ready. She felt the knot of nerves in her stomach wind tight.

Coco took a deep inhale. "What have I gotten myself into, Fredo?" Fredo looked at her, brown eyes dripping with affection. She rubbed his ears and kissed his head. "You're a great listener. If only you could talk." She pushed her tired body out of bed, walked to the bathroom, and stepped under the spray of hot water to wash the tension away.

It didn't help.

Coco's hair and body wrapped in Egyptian cotton, she walked past the luxurious creams pioneered by the Swiss dermatologists she worshipped and touted their benefit to her fans for years.

The daily hour-long skin hydrating ritual she'd religiously performed since she could remember seemed futile now. The same went for the five-mile runs to keep her tall body trim and shapely and everything she took to heart to keep her vanity and ego gratified.

Perfection was her trademark, her brand, had been since her teens. Now "was," was the operative word. Everything Coco valued seemed trivial now, but when you were handed life-altering news, priorities changed.

Taking a slow, contemplative look at herself in the mirror, Coco saw the rich green eyes the camera loved shadowed with worry, but she wouldn't bother with make-up. Coco wouldn't bother blow-drying the mink-coloured hair featured in the L'Oréal commercials women envied and spent thousands of dollars to mimic.

Towel drying her hair, Coco haphazardly bundled it into a wet ponytail and walked to her closet. Eyeing the hundreds of designer outfits and shoes she'd collected over the years, she opted for the Dolce & Gabbana jeans, a Chanel silk blouse, and the Manolo Blahnik black patent flats. Some of her glamorous image had to be upheld, she thought.

"Come on, Fredo, let's go get me some caffeine and you breakfast." Coco shrugged into her leather jacket and opened the front door. The air that hit her had a fall chill to it.

Stepping onto her front steps, she hugged her back for warmth and filled her lungs with cool air. It was six a.m., and the world was hushed with dawn, dreamlike. Coco feasted on the green, rolling hills that spread to the horizon. She thought that in her trek around the globe, she'd never seen anything more beautiful.

In the east, framing the landscape, a round, yellow sun arising for the day lit the outgoing dark sky. Trees clad in scarlet and gold painted the escarpment. High above her, Canada geese flew in V formation, their honks amplified by the peaceful silence.

Following the stone path that led to the resort, fallen leaves thickly carpeting the ground crunched at her feet. Coco smelled fall in the soft wind that ruffled the lingering leaves on trees that rose majestically toward the sky.

Fredo dashed ahead of Coco, and she watched him chase after a squirrel who easily outmaneuvered him by jutting up an elm tree.

"Come on, Fredo. Both you and I know you're not climbing that tree," Coco called out. Seeing the logic in that, Fredo gave the squired one last "we'll meet again" stare and darted toward Coco.

The walk from her home to the resort was a short ten minutes but invigorating.

Reaching the resort's back terrace, she climbed the stairs. Chairs were tilted against the round teak tables to ensure rain drained off, their padding stored for the winter. The colourful pumpkin-orange umbrellas, which shaded their occupants from the sun in the summer months, were collapsed and secured.

Coco waved at the four guests adventurous enough to be up this early. They warmed up in hoodies, tights, and running shoes to get their daily run in before the hiking trail filled up. Most of the resort's guests found comfort in the warmth of their beds until late morning and preferred to enjoy breakfast in the indoor dining room in front of the crackling fire in the hearth.

"Straight to the laundry room for your breakfast, Fredo. Don't you dare go into the kitchen and get in Chef's way, or you'll become today's lunch special," she said before opening the door.

In the pristine kitchen, Chef and her crew were busy with the breakfast preparation. Blenders whirred, juicers squeezed, freshly picked eggs sizzled in pans and knives chopped. The air was scented with baking bread, brewing Toraja Sulawesi coffee, and everything healthy the guests of Covington Spa expected during their ten-thousand-dollar three-day stay.

As steep as the price was, there was an eight-month wait for the privileged and bragging rights for the stay. That had come about from Coco's marketing ingenuity.

Those privileged enough to land on Covington Spa's guest list ranged from dignitaries to high-profile celebrities looking for a few days away from the spotlight. The spa provided guests anonymity, peace and quiet away from the flashing lights, the paparazzi, and fans for the duration of their stay.

Skirting Chef whom Coco didn't dare disturb with idle morning greetings or chitchat—one of Chef's kitchen rules you observed if you cherished your hearing—she crossed to the coffeemaker. Coco reached for the pot resting on the hot plate and filled her cup with steaming, black coffee. In complete silence, Coco walked past Chef through the sliding doors and onto the terrace.

Sipping coffee, Coco felt the wave of fatigue wash over her. She hadn't slept a wink in anticipation of what was coming. Since concocting the plan to deceive Emma and Mary into the reunion at the spa, Coco's nerves were wound as tight as a spring. Her heart hitched at the deception, but there was no way around it.

She'd made the wrong choice for what she thought was the right reason. The consequence of that mistake forced her to fade overnight from her two best friends' lives.

She hadn't contacted them in ten years, and that was deliberate, but she needed them now because those she'd considered friends, when push came to shove, turned out to be profiteers. The people in her life were in it to exploit her for who she was and her money.

Mary and Emma never would. They were stay-with friends. The type she could turn to no matter the hurt she'd caused.

There was pain, a terrible pain radiating out from Coco's chest, and she rubbed the heel of her hand against her breastbone to smooth it out. Blinking back the tears, she prayed things went her way today. Emma and Mary were the only friends she had left and her last recourse.

DR. MARY CARTER-TYRELL WASN'T UP for the spa weekend her husband, unexpectedly, surprised her with. She'd rather spend the three days at a medical conference furthering her intellect to benefit her intellect and patients rather than her vanity. Not to mention, the one-hour she spent driving to the luxurious spa was time from her life she'd never get back.

Her husband, however, thought otherwise and threatened divorce unless Mary took the weekend respite seriously.

"Pfft, as if you'll find anyone better than me," Mary pointed out to her husband of fifteen years.

"I won't. It's why I need you to take care of yourself. You need the time off. You're wound tight right now, Mary. If you don't do it for yourself, do it for me. I don't want my wife suffering a myocardial infarction."

Mary's frown turned to a grin. Her husband knew medical speak made her heart flutter, and she conceded. "Fine. I'll go."

Adam pressed his mouth to hers. "Good. The relaxing spa weekend will keep hypertension at bay and ensure your systolic and diastolic rates remain at ideal levels."

At that, Mary threw back her head and laughed.

FROM THE GRAVEL DRIVE, EMMA LOOKED around. The gentle roll of green hills dotted with wild purple Salvia. The pageant of autumn colour painted the trees bordering the property and the gardens hemming the house.

The air was ripe with the sounds and scents of rural life. Emma smelled pine, hay, horses, and the freshness brought on by green country living. She heard the bubbling brook, the neighing of horses, the song of cicadas, the call of birds, and the quack of ducks. High above her, she watched the hawk, wings spread wide, as he glided in a staggeringly blue sky.

Emma was a city girl at heart, but she couldn't escape relishing the comforting, rural sounds.

Emma's eyes turned to the rustic but dignified, two-story brick house. Late morning sunlight gleamed off the tall windows accented by white shutters. There were colourful Muskoka chairs and a swing at each end of the wrap-around porch with a heritage railing. From the tongue & groove porch ceiling, hanging flower baskets overflowing with trailing lobelia and pansies dripped with colour. Purple, lemon yellow, and watermelon red chrysanthemums along the flagstone path winked up at the sun.

Emma could see a whitewashed barn encased by a wood fence just as she'd seen in the movies. She heard the muffled sounds of laughter from women mounting horses followed by thudding hooves on dirt.

A directional sign TO SPA pointed to a newer, modern-looking building of poured concrete, steel and glass. Through the sparkling glass, Emma could see an indoor pool with its glistening blue water. Loungers were filled with women lounging the day away. A whirlpool with a visibly rising hot mist overflowed with chatty women sipping tropical drinks with tiny colourful umbrellas.

Signs directed guests to a gym and a hot yoga studio. A salon offered hand and stone massages, mani and pedis, facials, and hairstyling. All the pampering to melt away tension was there for Emma to take advantage of for three glorious days.

Emma felt her tightly wound knot of nerves loosen.

Covington Spa, the chi-chi poo-poo health resort ninety minutes north of her downtown Toronto home that she'd never heard of, was what she needed.

The weekend getaway, courtesy of AZ Travel, which she'd never heard of and at first thought it to be a hoax, couldn't have come at a better time. Emma didn't remember entering any contest. Still, she wasn't about to pass up the luxurious spa weekend retreat. Life wasn't on her side—it never seemed to be—and she deserved a bit of pampering.

With her canvass carry-on in hand, Emma walked up the walkway and stepped onto the porch. Walking around, the brown-haired Chihuahua sprawled at the top of the steps, eyeing her with a raised eye, her hand dropped to the brass handle. She pushed the front door open. The warmth that came at her was as comforting as the homey interior she stepped into.

Sunlight spearing from the large window above the entry door dappled the lobby's flagstone floor. Wood-beamed ceilings roofed the tall foyer. Reclaimed pine flooring, the colour of honey, sparkled. The floating, winding staircase led to the guest rooms on the second floor. In the fireplace fashioned of river rock, bursts of sparks crackled maple wood and scented the air.

Checking in at the front desk, Emma was welcomed and directed to the living room to wait until her deluxe room was readied. With the thought of the luxurious holiday floating on the brain, Emma walked into the cozy living room with long, plush couches, comfortable side chairs, and thick rugs.

She came to a stop when she saw them. Momentarily frozen and dazed, it took Emma a moment to process.

Aside from the shooting sparks and hissing fire from the hearth, the only sound Emma heard was her unsteady breathing. It had been years since, without explanation, they'd disappeared from her life.

Coco looked every bit the glamorous celebrity she'd become and Mary, the respectable doctor she was. In worn jeans and a T-shirt, Emma supposed she looked every bit the unassuming cashier she was. Emma never felt as if she fit into their swank lifestyle, and today was no exception.

"Hi, Emma." Coco put a smile on her face, walked to her, and embraced her. Surprise coursing through her system, Emma didn't reciprocate. "Welcome to Covington Spa."

It took Emma a second to associate the Covington name. "You own this spa."

"Yes," Coco said. Her eyes levelled with Emma's now she added, "The free weekend getaway was a ruse to get you here."

"A ruse?" Emma stared blankly at Coco. "Why?"

"I'm wondering the same thing. Why did you feel the need to get Emma and me here on false pretense, Coco?" Mary returned stiffly.

Coco didn't make eye contact and said nothing, but dodging, after all, was her M.O., Mary thought. Instead, Mary and Emma watched Coco swoop to the bar and slop brandy into her glass. The shaking hand that made the ice in her glass rattle when she tossed the drink back made something cold skitter up Mary's back while Emma felt the pleasure of her luxurious weekend dim.

Coming Soon

The Complete Woman
The Conflicted Woman
The Spiteful Woman
The Tortured Woman

The Relentless Woman Duology

The Relentless Woman
The Vindictive Women

The Unbreakable Woman Trilogy

The Unbreakable Woman
The Brave Woman
The Valiant Woman

Contact us

Email us at mllexiauthor@gmail.com to receive emails whenever M.L. Lexi publishes a new book. There is no charge or obligation and your information will remain confidential.

Visit us at www.mllexi.com to read excerpts of upcoming releases.